# SECRET KEEPER

## ALSO BY MITALI PERKINS

*Monsoon Summer*

*The Not-So-Star-Spangled Life of Sunita Sen*

*Rickshaw Girl*

**First Daughter Novels**

*White House Rules*
*Extreme American Makeover*

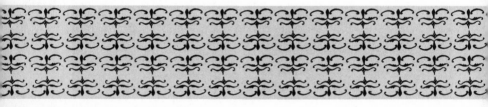

# SECRET KEEPER

## MITALI PERKINS

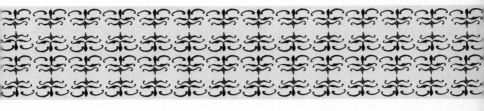

**DELACORTE PRESS**

Published by Delacorte Press
an imprint of Random House Children's Books
a division of Random House, Inc.
New York

Delacorte Press and colophon are registered trademarks of Random House, Inc.

Visit us on the Web! www.randomhouse.com/teens

Educators and librarians, for a variety of teaching tools, visit us at
www.randomhouse.com/teachers

*Library of Congress Cataloging-in-Publication Data*
Perkins, Mitali. Secret keeper / Mitali Perkins. — 1st ed.
p. cm.
Summary: In 1974 when her father leaves New Delhi, India, to seek a job in New York,
Asha, a tomboy at the advanced age of sixteen, feels thwarted in the home of her extended
family in Calcutta where she, her mother, and sister must stay, and when her father dies
before he can send for them, they must remain with their relatives and observe
the old-fashioned traditions that Asha hates.
ISBN 978-0-385-73340-3 (hardcover) — ISBN 978-0-385-90356-1 (lib. bdg.)
[1. East Indians—Fiction. 2. Sisters—Fiction. 3. Individuality—Fiction.
4. Family life—India—Fiction. 5. India—History—1947—Fiction.] I. Title.
PZ7.P4315Se 2009
[Fic]—dc22
2008021475

The text of this book is set in 12-point Eidetic Neo.

Book design by Cathy Bobak

Printed in the United States of America

10 9 8 7 6 5 4 3 2 1

First Edition

*For Sonali and Rupali*

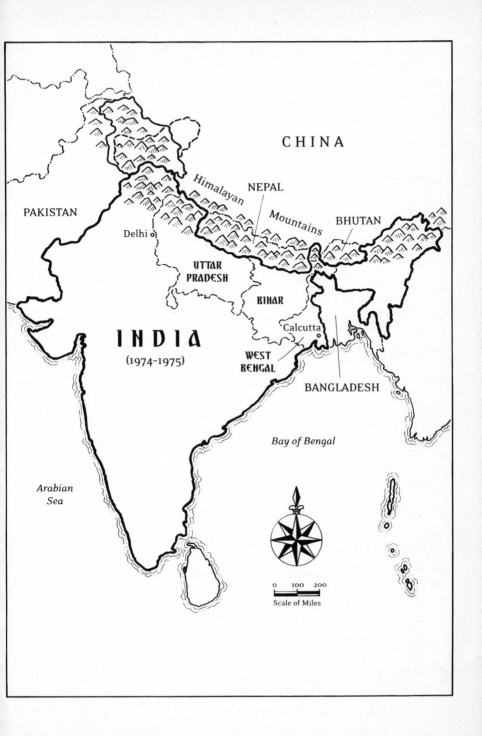

# ONE

Asha and Reet held their father's hands through the open window. The train picked up speed slowly, and Baba jogged, then ran alongside it. As his fingers slipped from their grasp, the girls turned and watched him dwindle and disappear into the Delhi haze.

"Watch your head, Osh!" Reet cried suddenly, pulling her sister inside before the train sliced into a tunnel.

The train swerved in the darkness, and Asha grabbed her sister's arm. Usually their mother would have issued the warning long before Reet had. But sometimes Ma was in the clutches of the Jailor, the girls' label for the heavy gloom that often fell over her like a shroud. Was she already so remote that the possibility of her daughter's decapitation couldn't rouse her?

When the train chugged out of the tunnel, Asha could

hardly believe what she saw. Their mother's face was buried in her hands, and tears—wet, salty tears—were staining her powdery cheeks in widening brown stripes.

What was happening? This had to be a mistake—there was no way Sumitra Gupta could be crying. The girls had seen their father get choked up many times, even while Ma or Reet sang about rain, grief, or heartache. But their mother never cried, retreating instead into stony silence that could last for hours, days, weeks. Even months, as it had after she'd read the telegram telling of her own mother's death.

But now Ma *was* crying. She was actually crying. The girls exchanged shocked looks. Then Reet sat down and gathered their mother in her arms.

Asha watched in amazement. This was *Ma,* who had ruled their household—and the entire social circle of Bengali families in Delhi—for years. To see her weeping on Reet's shoulder felt like watching a fortress crumble into a million pieces. And yet there was Reet—holding and comforting Ma as though their mother had become someone else altogether.

Asha sat down on the other side of her sister, an unusual sensation of pity softening her heart. Although she didn't touch Ma or say anything, she could feel the ache of missing Baba drawing them together.

She remembered Baba's last-minute request the night before: "If your ma gets like, well, like she does sometimes, I'm counting on you girls to lift her spirits. Promise me you'll take care of your mother and each other until you join me."

"We will, Baba," Reet had said, but her voice had sounded as doubtful as Asha felt.

"Keep this money and use it to buy her favorite sweets, Tuni," Baba had added, handing a small purse to Asha, who tucked it into her bag. Tuni was her childhood nickname, short for Tuntuni bird, the hero of a host of Bengali folktales.

Once the train was far out into the countryside, Ma pulled away from Reet's arms and sat up. She wiped the last trace of powder from her cheeks with one end of her saree and tucked loose wisps of hair back into her bun. "Forgive my sorrow, girls," she said in a low voice, still not looking at them. "I've only been away from your baba twice since our marriage day."

"We understand," Asha said.

Reet nodded. "This is the worst thing that's happened yet," she said, shifting the conversation from Bangla into English. The girls had fallen into the habit of speaking English to each other, like most Bishop Academy students. "Why couldn't we have all left for America together?"

"That would have been wonderful," Asha said wistfully. "I wouldn't have minded losing the flat, or selling the furniture, or even saying goodbye to the school if we could have gone to New York straightaway with Baba."

"Leaving school was hard, though, Osh," Reet said. "You looked heartbroken when Baba told us we couldn't afford the tuition anymore." Osh was Asha's nickname at school, and Reet had taken to using it. Asha, too, called her sister Reet, which was their schoolmates' way of shortening the more formal Amrita.

"Don't say anything about money in front of the relatives," Ma said sharply, sounding like herself again and yanking the conversation back into Bangla. "Your father will find a job soon; there's no use worrying your grandmother."

The word was that while England was flooded with Indian job candidates, American companies were just starting to hire foreign engineers. Asha only hoped that people all the way on the other side of the world realized that the Indian economy was in shutdown after months of strikes and protests, and that being jobless for four months wasn't Baba's fault. She wasn't sure she could survive a long stay in Calcutta with her father's side of the family. This would be their third visit from Delhi, the first without a scheduled departure date—and none of Baba's jokes to smooth over the tension.

Judging by the heavy silence, Reet and Ma were also imagining the bleakness of a Baba-less visit to Calcutta. One glance at Ma's face told Asha that the Jailor was threatening to close in again. Quickly she leaned forward, using Bangla so she could give her mother an honorific "you" to convey an extra measure of respect. "Why don't *you* tell us how you and Baba met, Ma? He tells his side, but we've never heard yours."

To Asha's relief, Ma nodded, slipped off her sandals, and settled herself into a cross-legged position. Their mother's toenails were painted pale pink, matching the tiny flowers embroidered on the border of her saree. Her sandals were gold, echoing the thread that made the silk shimmer with her graceful moves. She certainly looked the part of a

refined, prosperous, urban housewife; any traces of a village girl had disappeared long ago.

"We were visiting relatives in Calcutta," Ma started,
keeping her eyes fixed on the blur of rice paddies outside.
"One afternoon, I was on the veranda combing out my hair.
It was long then, down to my knees, and thick as a shawl. I
was singing; I remember the song still, it was a Tagore love
song I'd learned only weeks before."

She began to hum, and then sing in her low, rich voice:
"Light, my light, the world-filling light, the eye-kissing
light, heart-sweetening light! Ah, the light dances, my darling, at the center of my life; the light strikes, my darling,
the chords of my love; the sky opens, the wind runs wild,
laughter passes over the earth . . ."

The song trailed off, and Asha held her breath, motion-
ing to her sister to be still. After a few moments, their
mother gathered up the skein of the memory: "Suddenly I
felt somebody's eyes on me, and I turned quickly. There he
was, holding his briefcase and staring as though I was . . ."
The train entered another tunnel, and Ma faltered, losing
her place in the story.

"The 'queen of his dreams,'" Asha prompted in the
darkness. That was what Baba always called his wife. Asha
counted, one, two three, and then risked it: "What happened
next, Ma?"

"He fought for me," Ma responded immediately, gazing
at her reflection in the window. "His parents wept and
pleaded, but he wouldn't give in. They'd handpicked their
other daughter-in-law; she brought teak furniture, jewelry,
money, and sarees galore as her dowry, but they accepted

the two silk sarees and half a dozen gold bangles that *my* parents sent. What could they do? It didn't matter to their son that he'd graduated at the top of his class or that he was the son of an esteemed university professor, while I'd never gone to college. The second time I saw him, it was our wedding day. A bride is supposed to cry because she's leaving her parents, but I couldn't do it. Your baba had such love in his eyes as we exchanged garlands—"

The train burst into daylight again. Even though Asha flashed her sister a warning look, Reet interrupted Ma's story. "But what about leaving your parents? Wasn't that hard?"

Ma started, as though waking in the deepest part of a dream. She turned from the window, which was a square of sunshine now. "No use talking about the past," she said briskly. "That life is gone."

The conversation was over, but Asha could hardly believe that so much had been confessed. Her mother usually clung to secrets so tightly that nobody could pry them loose. Ma's face was regaining its usual composed, confident expression; the thought of her crying on Reet's shoulder seemed ridiculous now.

"I'm tired," Reet said suddenly, moving to the empty bench on the other side of the compartment.

Ma took out a finely knitted scarf from her bag and rolled it into a pillow. "Sleep, Shona," she said, passing the soft coil of wool to Reet.

"Shona" meant "gold" in Bangla, and it was what Ma and Baba had nicknamed their older daughter. They'd tried to train Asha when she'd first started lisping out words:

6

"Shona *Didi,* call her Shona *Didi.*" "Didi" was the standard address for an older sister. But Asha stayed with "Reet" through the years, leaving off the honorific "Didi" altogether.

Reet stretched out on the bench, hands palm to palm between cheek and pillow as always, and fell asleep almost immediately.

Baba had paid double to reserve all six places in the compartment. Asha overheard him talking to Ma: "You have to be more careful than ever since I won't be around. Especially while traveling with the girls overnight." Asha knew what he meant; her sister had been attracting unwanted attention from men for three or four years now, and it seemed to Asha that it was getting worse by the minute. Just last month, an older man had pressed himself behind Reet on a bus and refused to move, even after Baba had asked, courteously at first, then stridently after the man pretended not to hear. Eventually Baba had punched the man on the jaw, much to the girls' astonishment. They'd never seen their father that angry.

Asha stood up to make sure the door to their compartment was locked. Their father wasn't around to stop unwelcome visitors, so she was taking on the responsibility. All that would change once a telegram arrived from America with the best news in the world:

FOUND JOB STOP COME SOON STOP
LOVE, BABA STOP

# TWO

MA'S KNITTING NEEDLES BECAME RED-LOOPED BLURS, CLICK-ing and clacking to the rhythm of the train. She was making Baba a sweater for the cool spring nights in New York.

Asha felt herself relax; as long as Ma knit, she seemed better at keeping hold of her usual scolding self. Their mother, too, seemed to recognize the craft as a shield; her suitcase was stuffed with shawls and sweaters she was bringing as gifts to the relatives, designed and created in the long months since Baba had lost his job.

Asha sat back and looked out over fields drenched in sunlight. It was late April, the heart of the hot season, and cows, people, and stray dogs sought out patches of shade. Farmers, skin coal-black from hours in the sunshine, steered slow bullocks through rice paddies. Children raced each other, chasing tires with sticks down dirt lanes, ignoring the heat in the joy of play. Had her mother played like that in a village somewhere in the Himalayan foothills of North Bengal?

Ma had made the long trek back twice after her marriage, once after each of her parents had died, but had taken neither Baba nor the girls. As far as the sisters knew, they had no uncles or aunts on that side. The two of them tried to piece together a portrait of the Strangers, as they called their maternal grandparents, but Ma never revealed much. Baba couldn't answer their questions, either, claiming he knew little more than they did.

Quietly Asha reached into her bag and pulled out a fountain pen and a small leather-bound book secured with a lock. She was wearing the key on a long gold chain that she kept tucked under her salwar. With as little movement as possible, she carefully unlocked the book.

This was the fourth diary her father had offered her, and it had "S.K. 1974" printed on the cover in her neat handwriting. Only Asha and her sister knew that "S.K." stood for "secret keeper." The other three diaries, labeled "S.K. 1971," "S.K. 1972," and "S.K. 1973," were in the bottom of Asha's suitcase wrapped in an old sweater.

In "S.K. 1971" Asha had mostly scribbled about squabbles with her now best friend Kavita. That was the year they'd fought their way into real friendship. "S.K. 1972" was where Asha had raged after her body betrayed her for the first time. In "S.K. 1973" she wrote about tests and exams as an upperclassman at the academy, and the mad crushes she'd had on brothers Vijay and Anand Amritraj, Indian tennis stars.

In this diary "S.K. 1974," she'd already filled four months of pages with worries about money, concern over Baba's chain-smoking, and frustration during Ma's times of captivity in the clutches of the Jailor. It was also where she'd confessed her dream of what she wanted to do with her life. That entry was written just before she'd had to leave the academy in January, and she flipped to it now.

*January 10, 1974*

*I know what I'm going to be, S.K., I've finally decided. When Mrs. Joshi explained the science of psychology in class today, she must have put a spell on me. I was mesmerized. "Psychologists explore the mysteries of the human mind, girls," she told us. "A most valuable discipline. The challenge for Indians in the field is to master the best of Western theory and meld it with the realities of our own culture and society."*

*That's exactly what I want to do, I thought, as she kept talking. I could tell from the shivers on my skin that somehow I was designed for this job.*

*But India has only a few good programs here and there. Mrs. Joshi told me that I should probably think about going overseas to gain a foundation in the Western approach. The problem is that "good" Bengali girls like me don't leave the country alone to study.*

*What to do, S.K.?*

Her diary never answered her questions, but this time fate did. Right after that entry, Baba lost his job. Thanks to the economy shutting down, he couldn't find another in Delhi or Calcutta, so eventually the call for engineers in America seemed like the only option. This was the main reason Asha wasn't devastated about leaving India—in America, she'd still be under her parents' roof, and she could study whatever she wanted. Even the science of psychology.

Ma stopped knitting so that the blur of red became two white sticks and a patch of wool. "I don't see why your baba keeps giving you those diaries," she said.

Asha had mastered the art of locking a diary fast and slipping the key next to her skin; she didn't want Ma reading one word she'd written.

"They're like your knitting," she said. "Writing things out helps me survive."

"I don't know what you're talking about. Let me see it."

Reluctantly, Asha gave the diary to her mother, who fingered the leather, turned the book over, and tried to open it before handing it back.

"I still don't understand why you lock it. If I had my way, this nonsense would stop, but that father of yours lets you talk him into anything."

Asha stashed "S.K. 1974" safely in her bag. "That's the design of the book, Ma. It's supposed to be locked."

Ma shook her head. "You scribble for hours, Tuni. Wasting time when you could be learning to sing, or dance, or play the harmonium. You're sixteen now, and you have so few womanly accomplishments. Your grandmother blames me for it. She's been complaining in her letters about how hard it's going to be to find husbands for four grand-daughters."

"I'm going to college, Ma," Asha said, carefully not stressing the "I'm" so that her mother wouldn't take her words the wrong way. "Grandmother thinks that 'girls who get a good education find good husbands.'" Asha left off the "usually" that Grandmother emphasized when Ma was around, implying that her own daughter-in-law was the exception to the rule.

Ma sighed. "I've heard that from her a thousand times, but she won't pay for it. Don't count on any more schooling until your father finds a job, Tuni. It's too expensive."

"I'll study on my own, then," Asha said stubbornly, twisting the cap of her fountain pen.

"Isn't that the pen Kavita gave you?" Ma asked. "That girl pours out her parents' money like water."

"She's my best friend, Ma. She wanted to give me a nice goodbye present."

Ma snorted, but quietly, so that she wouldn't wake Reet. "She doesn't speak a word of Bangla. Couldn't sing a Tagore song if you paid her." This was one of the reasons Ma had never gotten to know Kavita well—Kavita was Punjabi and didn't speak the Holy Language, as the sisters called their mother tongue. Ma mingled only with other Bengalis who lived in Delhi, of the same class and caste as her husband's family.

"Who cares if she's Punjabi, Marathi, or Gujarati?" Asha asked. "Or even British for that matter? She's my friend."

"You'll forget about such so-called friends when you get married," Ma said, starting to knit again. "*I* don't need friends, do I? You two girls and Baba are my whole life."

Asha stifled a groan. She didn't want to be Ma's whole life. Or even one-third of it. But she knew from experience that arguing was useless. Her mother could never understand Asha's friendship with Kavita. It wasn't about competition and rivalry, the way middle-class Bengali housewives in Delhi interacted. Osh and Kavi rejoiced over each other's victories and suffered through each other's struggles. They ran around the academy courtyard during tea break, organizing games for their class until everyone who joined in was sweaty and laughing. Asha was going to miss practicing tennis and cricket in Kavi's family's enclosed garden; she was going to miss their long talks and laughter. But suddenly, in the face of Ma's certainty, Asha felt a twinge of doubt. Could even the closest of friendships stand the test of time and distance? Would Kavi vanish into Asha's past like Ma's childhood?

*No,* Asha told herself fiercely. *I'll never forget Kavi. And she'll never forget me. We'll be friends forever, just as we promised.* She tucked the pen into her bag next to the diary. She'd been stupid to take them out, even though she'd been longing to write ever since they got on the train.

Ma frowned at her red rectangle, holding it at a distance to find a dropped stitch. "That girl's a bad influence, anyway. I don't like how she gave you another tennis racket after I forbade you to play."

This time, it took Asha immense amounts of energy not

to debate her mother's point. She was battling the fury that always flamed when she remembered how Ma had given away her tennis racket and cricket bat to the servants. The bat was cheap, and Baba had bought another just like it, but the racket was an irreplaceable wooden Chris Evert from America, and Asha had won it as a first prize in a tournament. She would have liked to keep it forever as a memory of playing tennis with Baba. And trouncing boy after boy while he watched.

Their father had learned tennis when he'd studied engineering in London, and he joined a club in Delhi after he and Ma settled there as newlyweds. He'd started teaching Asha when she was seven, and she'd learned so fast that Baba encouraged her to start playing competitively. He and Reet stood at the sidelines cheering, and people came from miles around to witness the unusual sight of a girl winning matches in an all-boy juniors league. An Indian Billie Jean King or Virginia Wade, they called her. Or Vijaya, the female version of the name Vijay, after the more famous Amritraj brother, who the past year had actually made it all the way to the quarterfinals at Wimbledon. Asha and Baba had listened to the matches on the radio, shouting like maniacs every time Amritraj hit a winner.

Asha played tennis for five years, until the day she'd woken her sister in a panic after finding rust-colored stains in her underwear. Everything changed with her body on that day, and there was no going back. Asha could no longer wear shorts or pants—only salwar kameez and her school uniform. She'd had to start growing her hair. No more going down the hill to the market with Baba or playing cricket with Kavi and the neighborhood boys in the street. And worst of all, it wasn't *proper* for a young woman to play tennis with boys at the club.

When Ma issued her final edict about tennis, Asha had lost her temper, shouting at her mother with the servants in earshot. Baba had taken his younger daughter into another room, closed the door, and delivered an unusually stern lecture. She'd listened quietly, her anger spent.

"It's my fault, Tuni," Baba ended. "Ma's right; I've spoiled you and it's time I faced facts. But even so, I will not permit you to talk to your mother like that. Ever."

Baba so rarely laid down the law that Asha always obeyed when he did.

"I don't know how Punjabi parents train their daughters," Ma said now, needles battling each other like swords again. "But in a good Bengali home, a girl obeys her mother. Especially while other people are around."

Asha was still swallowing anger over losing her racket, her tennis, and her freedom. And now maybe even her friendship with Kavi.

"Did you hear me, Tuni?" Ma asked. "Do not bring shame to me or your father in your grandmother's house."

Asha took a deep breath. "I'll try, Ma," she made herself say, but the words took a mighty effort, and only the memory of her father's face allowed her to mean them.

# THREE

THE TRAIN MOVED STEADILY SOUTHEAST FROM THE STATE OF Uttar Pradesh and through the plains of Bihar, finally reaching the state of West Bengal by the time morning came. It was drawing closer to the neighboring country of Bangladesh, where three years earlier a war between India and Pakistan had devastated homes and farms and villages. The suffering, along with countless refugees, still spilled across the border.

Asha woke first and peered through the window. The villages they passed were crowded, the houses more makeshift, and even the cows looked skinnier. The tea sellers who boarded the train during the stops at the stations began speaking Bangla instead of Hindi.

Asha and Reet staggered down the aisle to the bathroom. They took turns grasping each other's hands for support as they squatted and swayed over the hole in the floor and washed themselves thoroughly. At the small sink, they brushed their teeth and splashed their faces with cold water.

Back in the compartment, Ma had folded up the benches and was repacking her handbag. "We have to put on our sarees, Shona," she said, shutting and latching the door. "Tuni, block the view."

Asha held a shawl across the window as Ma and Reet redraped and tucked the long pieces of silk around their bodies. The span of Ma's still-slender waist was almost as narrow as Reet's, and their tight blouses clung to their matching curves. Ma's saree was pink and Reet's was blue and brand-new, a splurge made to ensure her grand Calcutta entrance.

Watching the painstaking ritual, Asha was glad that Ma had let her wear a salwar kameez. She'd worn sarees to parties for the past couple of years, but she still didn't feel comfortable swathed in six and a half yards of material. Her green, embroidered traveling salwar kameez was soft, the way she liked it, and there was nothing rounded in sight. Not that she was hiding anything out of sight, either, a fact that didn't worry her much.

"That's why I'm fast on the tennis court and the cricket pitch," she said when Ma moaned about her younger daughter's slowly changing physique.

"What good is that since you no longer play sports," Ma retorted.

"I do play sports, in the garden with Kavita."

"I don't see why your father allows you to do that."

"We stay behind the walls, Ma, nobody sees us."

And so it went. Asha overheard a couple of Ma's Delhi friends murmuring about how tough it was going to be to marry off a "skinny, underdeveloped girl" like Sumitra's younger daughter. Apparently a girl had to fill a bra of decent cup size to attract a husband.

*That's good for me,* Asha thought, her arms getting tired from holding the shawl across the window. *More time to be free. Get my PhD. Do what I really want.*

In America, where women were burning bras and fighting for equal rights, they didn't need curves to snare a husband. Sixteen-year-old American girls could play sports, drive cars, win scholarships, keep studying, even think about staying unmarried if they wanted.

Asha Gupta, tennis champion.

Asha Gupta, psychologist.

Asha Gupta, forever.

Once the sarees were draped to satisfaction, Reet combed Asha's hair and fixed it in a fresh, tidy braid. Ma tried three different hairstyles on Reet before settling on a thick bun that coiled on the top of her head like a crown. Finally Ma combed out her own long hair, arranged it exactly like Reet's, and powdered her face again carefully.

When the train pulled into Calcutta's Howrah station, Ma made them wait until a knock sounded at the compartment door. "Open! Hurry up!" said a voice that sounded so much like her father's that Asha's heart skipped a beat. But then Reet unlatched the door, and there stood a stockier, grimmer version of Baba—Uncle, head of the clan and master of the home where the two Gupta boys had been raised.

Reet started to welcome him with the traditional greeting for elders, bending to touch his feet with her hands and then tapping her own forehead, but Uncle stopped her before she could complete the whole pronam. "The train is only stopping for a few minutes," he said. "We have to disembark quickly. I've hired a coolie to bring the heavy bags."

He didn't seem to speak directly to Ma. It would have been wrong for him to speak freely to his sister-in-law, so that wasn't unusual. But Uncle went beyond that; Asha had noticed it during their last visit, even though she'd been only twelve then. He hardly even looked at Ma. It was as if he didn't trust his gaze to find his younger brother's wife for a second.

The girls and Ma gathered their handbags and followed Uncle to the platform. There he paused briefly to permit the reunion ritual, placing his hands on his nieces' heads as they touched his feet. Asha turned away as Ma bent before her brother-in-law. Something in her hated to see Ma, proud and strong, bending in front of a man who wasn't Baba. Of course Ma never gave Baba pronam in greeting—only elderly women still gave their husbands such a traditional sign of submission. Every decent Bengali woman, though, was expected to honor her older brother-in-law with this gesture, and Ma offered it as gracefully as she had four years earlier.

Uncle received Ma's pronam with his face averted. "Taxi's waiting," he grunted, hurrying them along the crowded platform. A thin, agile, red-turbaned coolie followed them, three suitcases stacked on his head.

The beggars descended once the Gupta family left the

platform and entered the station. In the prosperous neighborhood where the girls had lived in Delhi, a few beggars used to wander the streets, but they were nothing compared to the multitude of refugees crowding Howrah station. Faces covered with sores, hair matted and straw-yellow from malnutrition, hoisting bony babies on their hips, they wailed or whined about their plight to everyone and anyone.

"Stay together," Uncle called.

Asha kept her eyes on his broad back. He was striding forward, elbowing people aside and scolding them to make room. Reet clutched Asha's hand, and Ma stayed so close behind, she kept stepping on the heels of their sandals.

"Ma," Reet said over her shoulder. "Can't we give them something?"

"Are you insane?" Ma hissed. "If you give one of them anything, the rest will mob us."

Asha held her breath. Beggars were pressing so tightly against her, she felt as if she were inhaling the air coming from their mouths. They finally reached the taxi, and the driver flung open the door to the backseat. Ma pushed Reet in first, then Asha, and then gathered her saree and jumped inside before Uncle slammed the door. He stayed outside to make sure their bags were deposited in the cab and to pay the coolie.

Countless hands tapped and pounded the windows of the hot, enclosed taxi. Ma covered her head with the loose end of her saree and leaned her forehead against the back of the driver's seat.

Asha couldn't help seeing the faces outside. What were

their stories? What were their secrets? Did they have places or people to keep them safe?

One of the beggars pressed an open hand on the window next to Reet, and Reet put her own hand on the glass from the inside. Finger to finger, she positioned her palm until the window became a mirror for the two girls' hands.

Asha watched the expression on the beggar's face outside change and relax until something in it seemed familiar. *She looks like a younger version of Ma,* Asha realized in amazement, as Reet and the girl exchanged grins.

Both hands stayed against the glass until the cab pulled away.

Just as he had last time, all the way to the house, Uncle complained about traffic and barked out directions at the cabdriver. It hurt Asha to hear his voice, so much like Baba's and yet so different. Four years earlier Baba had been there, chatting with that driver, finding out about his family and what village he came from, asking how and when he'd found his way to the city. Now only Uncle's voice could be heard; this driver responded with grunts and monosyllables as he maneuvered through streets full of police cars, skinny cows, and people picketing.

The house was in a quiet suburb in the southern outskirts of the city. During the war of independence from British rule in 1947, Asha's grandparents had fled across the border with their two young sons and spent their savings to buy it. A few of the fancier houses in the neighborhood were well maintained, making the Guptas' three-story building look shabby in comparison. Uncle's income as a manager in a chemicals factory provided enough for the family's living expenses and covered tuition fees for his son and two daughters, but it didn't cover luxuries like home improvements. Grandmother had counted on Baba's monthly contributions from Delhi to pay for any repairs and to tuck away some small savings. Four months earlier, of course, that extra money had stopped coming.

Uncle argued over the cab fare as if every penny counted. Last time, Asha remembered, Baba had left the driver grinning over a big tip.

"I'm late for work," Uncle said as he hurried past them into the house. "Your aunt and grandmother are waiting inside."

Reet held the gate open. The driver left the suitcases beside them, jumped in his cab, and pulled away. The high iron gate clanged shut.

Asha stared up at the three-story house that still looked run-down since her visit four years before. A path wound through a long garden and led to a screened-in veranda. There were two narrow yards on either side, one with smoke rising from a garbage pile and laundry hanging on a line, the other squeezed between the Gupta house and the large, newly painted house next door.

Coconut and banana trees blocked the sunshine on every side except the front, the windows on the first floor were secured with bars, and the property was completely fenced in. As they waited by their bags, Asha couldn't help feeling she was about to serve a sentence for a crime she hadn't committed.

# FOUR

A SERVANT WALKED TOWARD ASHA, REET, AND MA, BOWED HIS head slightly in greeting, and took two suitcases inside. Briefcase in hand, Uncle strode back down the path and out the gate again. "I'll be back in time for tea," he informed them, and was gone before they could respond.

A voice called from somewhere inside the house. "Come in, come in; don't worry about that last suitcase, the servant will bring it!"

The girls and Ma left their sandals with the pile of shoes strewn across the veranda. Asha squinted inside the dim house. Two sets of wide eyes peered at her from either side of a saree-clad figure. The saree belonged to Auntie and the eyes to the twins, who came from behind their mother shyly to greet the older cousins they hardly remembered.

The wife of the oldest Gupta brother was showing her age by the thickening of her figure and lines deepening from nose to mouth. Asha caught the envy in Auntie's eyes as they studied Ma's smooth skin and hair still as dark as a crow's feathers. Would she exchange her status as older wife or her educated, prosperous background for a share of Ma's allure?

Auntie and Ma embraced; no exchange of pronam was necessary between the daughters-in-law of the house. They were supposed to be on equal footing while Grandmother was alive, but during their last visit it had been clear that Auntie was eager to exercise her power as wife of the head of the home.

Grandmother came bustling out of the kitchen, wiping her hands on her white cotton saree. Wives like Ma and Auntie painted red stripes along the parts in their hair and wore bangles on both wrists, but Grandmother followed the custom of avoiding colors or extra adornment prac-ticed by widows for generations. *She* was a widow of char-acter, not like the one that Ma and her friends had gossiped about in their Delhi neighborhood, a childless woman who continued to wear lipstick, high heels, and a rainbow of colors after her husband died. It made Asha fu-rious that a man was free to remarry after his wife's death while a widow faced a lifetime of white sarees, fasting from meat and fish, and endless praying. Asha had always secretly imagined the young Delhi widow finding a new love.

"That terrible cook!" Grandmother was saying. "I told

her you'd be hungry, and she didn't start frying the luchis till just now. Poor Bontu had to leave for office without eating anything."

Bontu was Uncle's nickname, and even though he was middle-aged, married, and the father of three children, Grandmother still fussed over him as though he were a schoolboy. Neither of her sons could do wrong in her eyes. Bintu was her nickname for Baba, and if anything, she seemed to dote on her younger son even more than she did on his brother.

After receiving her granddaughters' pronam, Grandmother took Asha's chin and tilted it up with her fingertips. "Looks just the same, even though she's a woman now," she announced, letting go and shrugging. "She'll never be a beauty, this one."

Asha felt as though she'd been slapped. Her own grandmother telling her how ugly she was? She couldn't remember being appraised like this during their last visit. But of course she had been a child then, not a *woman.*

Grandmother turned to Asha's sister, eyes lingering on Reet's face and shape, taking in the sight as though she'd just lifted the lid of a velvet box. "And how is the pearl of the family?" she asked, stroking Reet's cheek. "So lovely! So fair!"

Asha's hands clenched and unclenched as she fought to control her tongue. At Bishop Academy, their teachers warned the girls not to focus on outside appearances. "Character," students were taught. "Wisdom. Discipline. Courage. Those are the true womanly qualities that stand the test of time." Asha's fierce determination to succeed had won the admiration of teachers and students alike. But the feminine attributes that seemed to count in her paternal grandparents' house had always been skin-deep. And she obviously didn't have enough of them.

"I'm fine, Grandmother," Reet was saying. "You look just the same as you did four years ago, and so does Auntie, but who are these huge creatures?"

She ruffled the hair of the cousins, who were clustering around her. Sita and Suma were twins, not identical but plain and dark-skinned and skinny, just like Asha.

"Where's Rajiv?" Ma asked. Rajiv was the one cousin who was close to their age, and the only boy of the house. He was seventeen, like Reet, and the girls called him Raj for short.

"At college, of course," Auntie answered proudly. "He studies so hard, that boy."

"Not hard enough," Grandmother added, acknowledging Ma's pronam with a nod. "Lazy, that one is. And his father so hardworking, too!" Her eyes raked over her older daughter-in-law as though she knew exactly where the laziness in her grandson's character originated.

"He's a good boy, your son," Ma told Auntie. "Has he put on some weight? He was always so thin."

She was using proper Bangla, polished and beautiful, just as she had with the Bengali families in their Delhi social circle. When it was just the four of them at home, Ma slipped into an odd, nasal pronunciation and slang village words that Baba and the girls understood but didn't use themselves. To Asha's ears, the public version sounded as if her mother were acting; her at-home Bangla was sweeter and easier to obey.

"I feed my son plenty of food," Auntie answered, obviously taking Ma's words personally. "He's growing up nicely."

Suma, the more verbal of the twins, piped up. "He plays cricket all the time. We never see him studying."

"Hush!" Auntie snapped. "Don't talk about your brother like that."

Suma's face fell at her mother's rebuke.

"*My* boys were always top of their class," Grandmother said. "A woman's greatest duty and privilege is to see that her son succeeds."

Auntie glowered at Grandmother's correction, and Ma flinched almost imperceptibly as she took the jab at her son-less status. Asha and Reet exchanged glances. The cousins had grown, the tight bun of hair on Grandmother's head was almost completely gray, and Auntie had put on a few pounds. Otherwise, things were just as they remembered— the air simmering with tension between Grandmother and her daughters-in-law, competition between the wives as thick as luchi dough. And this time, there was no Baba to make the peace.

# FIVE

Reet and Asha were sharing a room with Sita and Suma until Baba sent for them. It had no door; only a curtain for privacy. Their cousin Raj had a small room to himself, with a door to shut. *Lucky bum,* Asha thought. *Gets a space of his own just because he's got different body parts than we do.*

All four granddaughters were expected to sleep together, stacked sideways across the same bed under one large mosquito net. It was the bed that Baba and Uncle had shared when they were boys. *Probably the same mosquito net, too,* Asha thought, feeling almost as desperate for privacy as the beggars in Howrah station were for food.

The household's daily routine left hardly any time for solitude. After breakfast, Uncle headed to work and Raj to college. Grandmother bustled in and out, ordering the servants around and taking one small granddaughter on her lap at a time to comb out and braid her hair. Once the twins left for school, the three older women gathered in the living room to knit and embroider, staying under the fans as the heat intensified. Ma made it clear that Reet and Asha were expected to join them.

While Reet entertained by singing or gossiping about the latest film celebrities, Asha curled up in a corner of the room and read. She'd brought along a few favorites from her childhood: her dog-eared copy of *Grimms' Fairy Tales*, a few of Enid Blyton's books, and E. Nesbit's *The Enchanted Castle, The Railway Children,* and *Five Children and It.*

Thankfully, here in Calcutta, her professor-grandfather's glassed-in bookcase was stocked with Shakespeare, Dickens, Milton, and Trollope. Asha was working her way through them, though some weren't easy reads. His wise, loving presence in the house was growing as dim as the light filtering through the banana leaves, and she liked the way the books connected her to him.

An hour or so before noon, Auntie would rouse herself and head to the kitchen to oversee the preparation of lunch for her husband and son. A man on a cycle waited outside for tin containers full of steaming rice and fish curry and lentils that he delivered to Uncle's office and Raj's college. Shortly after that, the younger cousins came home, and then the house grew still as Auntie, Ma, Reet, and Grandmother rested and the little girls napped.

That was when Asha seized her chance. Taking her diary, she tiptoed up the stairs to the roof and closed the door quietly behind her. The flat cement roof was enclosed on all four sides by a low wall. Asha walked to the front of the house and looked down on the large field across the road. From the opposite wall, she glimpsed a pond behind a banyan tree, and the cricket fields and buildings of her cousin's college in the distance. To the sides were the neighbors' houses, one higher and the other lower. The afternoon sky stretched overhead from horizon to horizon, and when Asha looked up, she felt as if she were in a quiet, hot balloon. Even the crows were resting from the heat of the day.

Tall coconut trees between their house and the taller house next door provided a bit of shade, and Asha sat cross-legged in the biggest patch of it. Finally she was alone, and she inhaled huge breaths of sunlight and open air. The atmosphere was thick and wet, making sweat pour down her neck into every nook of her body, but Asha didn't care. She started writing.

> *Oh, it's good to have some privacy. Being constantly scrutinized by Auntie and Grandmother is like having three mas around. Why do they have to comment constantly about how I look, S.K.? I've been called "dark" and "skinny" so many times, the words should lose their sting, but somehow they don't. What's wrong with being dark, anyway? Or being thin? I know the answer, of course: It hinders my chances of snaring a good husband. What would those protesting women who burn their bras in America say about THAT, I wonder?*
>
> *Which leads me to my next complaint: still no*

*telegram from Baba. What is taking him so long?*
*The job market for engineers in America was*
*supposed to be ten times better than in Delhi. After*
*only a few weeks, Grandmother's already hinting*
*about the extra cost of having us here, and Reet*
*and I are starting to worry about Ma, who gets*
*quieter by the day.*

*And me? I'm about to explode from boredom*
*and frustration. It's so HOT. And there's NOTHING*
*to do. If only there were someone INTERESTING to*
*talk to besides Reet. Raj hasn't said a word to us*
*since we got here. He looks so different now that*
*he's shaving, and he has a new, deep voice, which*
*we only get to hear when he answers his parents.*
*Otherwise, he disappears into his room to study,*
*then meets his friends to play cricket or tennis. I*
*hear them laughing and joking, just like Kavi and I*
*used to.*

Asha paused to flick the sweat from the crook of her elbow. Suddenly she caught sight of a face staring at her through the coconut leaves. It was on the fourth story of the house next door, only a few feet away from the Guptas' roof. Even as she turned, though, the shutters closed and the face disappeared, leaving behind an impression of an intense gaze.

The stately four-story house and garden next to the Guptas' was the most expensive property in the neighborhood. The family who used to live there had moved to England since Asha's last trip to Calcutta and someone else had taken over. *Someone who likes to spy on other people,* Asha thought, frowning. She shrugged and kept writing, irritated by her lack of privacy even up here.

*There's absolutely no place to be alone in this house. Otherwise known as my prison. If only I could leave for school like Raj and the little girls! I studied like a slave and passed my O levels with flying colors, but what good does that do me now? I'll have to take one more year of high school in America—that's what they call higher secondary. And then, university, to study whatever I want to study and be whatever I want to be.*

*Oh, it's terrible not to have money. It's not that I miss being rich, it's that I hate how POWERLESS you are without some rupees tucked away. We used up most of our savings to buy Baba's airplane ticket, so what's the difference between the four of us and those beggars at Howrah station? Nothing except that we have relatives who let us stay with them, and the hope that Baba can find a good job. Oh, and two untouchable dowries in the Gupta family safe at the bank, jewelry and a bit of money, kept with Suma's and Sita's so that the four of us have a prayer of marrying decently.*

"Osh, time for tea!" Reet's voice called from the stairwell below.

Asha locked her diary and tucked the key back under

her salwar kameez. She didn't want anybody other than her sister to start asking questions regarding her whereabouts. Just before she left the roof, she noticed that the shutters of their neighbor's fourth-story room were slightly ajar, as though someone had opened them just enough to see and not be seen.

Male voices joined the conversation over tea, as Uncle and Raj returned from work and college. The little girls grew tired of paper dolls and begged their cousin to read them a story. Asha always agreed. She had been one of Bishop Academy's elocutionary stars, and had inherited Baba's flair for timing and delivery. Ma, Grandmother, Reet, and Auntie would stop chattering while she read aloud or told a story. Even Uncle and Raj listened.

Fairy tales were her favorite read-alouds; she'd analyzed her love for them in her diary. Was it because evil was always vanquished at the end? Was it because the most unlikely characters stuck in the worst quandaries sometimes got their happy endings? She loved the Bengali folktales, too, and their version of a rakosh, or monster, which was usually slain by a weak underdog—the runt of a family, the village fool, or even a small bird named Tuntuni.

Conscious of her small cousins taking in the fairy tales with wide eyes, Asha did the same sort of editing that she did silently for herself. She had developed the skill of sending her eyes skimming two or three sentences ahead of her voice. Without skipping a beat, she replaced phrases like "the most beautiful girl in all the kingdom" with "the sweetest and kindest girl in all the kingdom," left out as much description as she could of female physical attributes, and completely obliterated words and phrases like "fair" and "white skin." Nobody listening seemed to notice, and Asha figured the Grimm brothers wouldn't mind. Their princesses and peasant girls got slightly more noble, smart, generous, and brave, and less physical, that was all. The Tuntuni stories she could tell just as Baba had told her. They didn't need editing because the bird's success didn't rely on looks but on clever tactics.

"Another one, another one!" the twins clamored when Asha was finished.

"Asha needs to drink her tea," Reet told them. "Another one tomorrow."

Asha took the steaming cup from her sister. "Uncle, who lives in the house next door?" she asked.

"Man named Sen bought the place. Family used to own a big jute farm in the village. Sold it for a fortune. Hear he and his wife like to play cards; we've been meaning to ask them to dinner. One son, but we don't see much of him."

"It's a sad story," Auntie said, with the relish of someone in the know. "Apparently the son's quite odd. Shone at university but refused to practice medicine or study engineering. Spent a year in Europe doing who knows what. Now he stays in his room day and night and hardly mixes with anybody. Of course he doesn't need a job because their family's so rich." She reached over to ruffle Raj's hair fondly. "Not like my boy, who has to support all of us someday."

Raj pulled away from her touch, slumping even lower in his chair.

"Such a waste," Grandmother added, sighing. "A lovely inheritance and an only son. But he's mad, that one."

Asha noticed that Ma, who was staring out the window into the garden, wasn't participating in the family gossip session.

"Here comes the Jailor," Reet muttered to Asha as the family's conversation shifted. "She hates being here so much. And she misses Baba."

Uncle turned up the radio to catch Prime Minister Indira Gandhi's speech defending herself against accusations of corruption. He was a big supporter of Gandhi, the daughter of Jawaharlal Nehru, who had helped lead India to independence during Uncle's boyhood.

As Mrs. Gandhi promoted her "Abolish Poverty" program in a loud, forceful voice, Asha wanted to cheer. "We've got a woman in charge of our country," she said to her sister. "Why can't she share some power with the rest of us?"

Reet sighed. "It's women who make it harder on other women. Haven't you noticed? Grandmother's always criticizing Ma, and Auntie makes snide comments about 'rustic traditions' passed down from the other side of our family."

"I wish Ma would stand up for the Strangers," Asha said. "I would do it myself but I don't know anything about them."

"We know they didn't have much money."

"Money," Asha said, her tone of disgust making the word sound like a curse. "It's the real head of this home, isn't it?"

They couldn't help seeing Uncle frowning over the bills, which must be higher than ever with three extra mouths to feed. And now that Baba wasn't sending anything Grandmother's way, the family's only savings had dwindled to what was in the four girls' dowries. What would happen in case of an emergency?

Grandmother's answer was to chant loud prayers for Baba's job in front of the household idols. When that happened, Ma quickly picked up her knitting. Baba's third sweater was almost finished; the first two had already been packaged and shipped to New York.

"When will Baba send for us, Osh?" Reet asked wistfully.

"Soon, I'm sure. He won't let us down. Has Raj said more than three words to you yet?" Asha asked, watching their cousin gulp his hot tea as quickly as he could.

"No," Reet answered. "He's gone totally mute."

As though he knew he was the subject of his cousins' whispered conversation, Raj put his empty cup down, grabbed his cricket bat, and left the house. Uncle switched off the radio and followed, heading out to the market hand in hand with his two daughters to buy food for the next day. Grandmother, Auntie, and Ma shifted to the kitchen to supervise the cook's preparation of dinner.

Reet and Asha stayed in the living room, alone for a change. "What's Raj's problem, anyway?" Asha asked her sister, using her normal speaking voice now that the coast was clear.

"Hees bod-ee eez chang-ink," Reet said, sounding like the Russian science teacher in Delhi who introduced every student to the mysteries of human development. Thanks to stronger-than-ever ties to the Soviet Union, Indian schools were constantly receiving outdated Russian textbooks, clunky typewriters, and even ancient teachers from Moscow. Bishop Academy girls liked to mimic Mrs. Roubichev's accent when they chatted about "forbidden topics."

"He hasn't changed that much," Asha said. "He's just taller and skinnier. And he has four mustache hairs now."

"He was only thirteen the last time we visited, Osh. *Our* bodies have changed since then. I think we make him uncomfortable now."

Asha stood and began pacing the room. "Mine hasn't changed that much," she said. "I'm taller and skinnier, too."

"You are a voo-man now, darlink," Reet told her sister. "Vether you like it or not."

"Don't remind me. I wish *I* could go out and play cricket. My arms and legs are turning into Chinese noodles."

During their time in Calcutta, neither sister had stepped outside the house once. They were learning fast that their family's social circle and neighborhood were even more conservative than they had been in Delhi. Girls their age didn't walk down the street unless they were with their elders or heading to school in a crowd of classmates. Reet didn't seem to mind, but Asha did.

"We're still on our own, at least for a while," Reet said

sympathetically. "Why don't you climb the stairs a few times? I'll keep count."

Asha managed to dash up and down the stairs ten times before Grandmother came bustling in to locate the source of "all that noise."

# SIX

*It's happened, S.K. This town has discovered my sister.*

*Yesterday the whole family went to the cinema, the first time Reet and I escaped the house. When we walked back after the film, people actually came out on balconies and verandas to watch us. To watch REET.*

*Within a half an hour, a gang of male idiots had gathered on the corner outside our house, laughing, chatting, even hooting and catcalling up at our window. And they wouldn't leave.*

*Uncle didn't quite know how to handle the situation, so he decided to ignore it. If Baba had been here, he'd have stormed outside and made those fools leave, just like he did that time a boy* followed Reet home from college—the third time I've ever heard him raise his voice, along with that day the geezer tried to grope Reet, and when he scolded me for shaming Ma.

The strange thing is that Auntie's teasing MA about this crazy turn of events. And Ma's suddenly all talkative again. Who could have guessed that here in Calcutta, a sudden outbreak of male interest in Reet could defeat the Jailor? Well, at least now we've got three things on our side: Baba, Knitting, and a bunch of Lusting Idiots.

"Boys used to gather outside my house when I was Reet's age," Ma told Auntie and Grandmother. "They'd sing love songs and toss flowers into my room until midnight."

She's never told Reet and me this detail about her history. She brings out something from her past only when she wants to flaunt it in front of women who obviously aren't jealous enough of her already. As if it's some kind of trophy to have a bunch of drooling fools outside your window.

The only dunderhead who stares at me is the Odd Hermit next door. I thought I'd found my sanctuary here on the roof but he's ten tiny meters away, and even though I'm trying to pretend he's not there I can feel his eyes on me right now. Why doesn't he ogle Reet like the rest of them? One more bean in her pile wouldn't matter much; he's as irritating as one pea under twenty-five mattresses.

*I think I'll go mad living in this house. I can't
even sweat away my frustration like I used to in
Delhi. Come ON, Baba. Send that telegram!*

While the house was still quiet, Asha went downstairs
to talk to Reet, who was stretched out on the bed reading a
magazine beside the sleeping twins.

"Do you think I could head outside and take a walk?"
Asha asked. "Nobody's actually told us we can't. Not in
Calcutta, anyway."

"You may as well try," Reet said, yawning. "I'd go with
you, but it's too hot. Besides, there may be lunatics out
there who can't take their eyes off *these*." She scowled down
at her breasts as though they were her enemies.

"They're like a bunch of hungry calves who see an ud-
der," Asha said. "Wonder what would happen if I put on one
of your bras and stuffed a couple of mangoes inside? Would
they ogle me, too?"

"Of course. They don't care if these are real or not—at
least not till their wedding night."

"Disgusting," said Asha.

She was tempted to play the prank, but maybe another
day. Staying inside her own shape for now would provide
the freedom from attention she needed to get to the market
and back before tea. She'd promised Baba to buy some
sweets for Ma, and she had to keep her word, didn't she?

She found the small purse of money Baba had given her,
crept downstairs and through the living room, and made
her way into the veranda, where she slipped on her sandals.

Then she hurried down the path and out the gate. Inadvertently, she glanced up at the house next door, but there was no sign of her prying neighbor. You couldn't see his window from anywhere except their roof and the side garden, she realized; the coconut trees almost completely blocked the view.

Striding down the lane, Asha let herself enjoy the feel of sunshine on her skin, the caress of the breeze in her hair, and the sound of her own heart beating faster than normal. A few men walked toward her, but none paid her any attention. *No mangoes in sight*, she thought.

Vendors at the corner market were starting to set out wares for the afternoon shoppers. Beggars gathered there, too, and a small girl held out her palm, making the whimpering, wheedling sounds she'd probably been taught by the person who sent her into the streets. Asha opened the purse, shook out the loose poisha inside, and gave it all to the girl, figuring that Baba wouldn't mind if she used only the rupee notes.

Keeping her money hidden, she bargained expertly with the sweetshop owner, just as Ma did in a saree shop, and returned at a fast clip carrying a dozen freshly made, top-quality panthuas in a covered clay bowl. Just before entering the gate, she turned to glower at the four or five young men gathered across the way. Had she imagined the pair of binoculars one of them was whisking out of sight?

Ma met Asha on the veranda, and the scolding started there. "You went out alone," she admonished, pulling Asha inside the house. "A girl of your age! What kind of a mother will they think I am? I hope nobody saw you. Eesh!"

If Asha had to choose one word in the Bangla language to abolish, it would be "eesh." That single syllable, pronounced with just the right intonation, brought with it a twist of shame and loss and disappointment that Asha could never fully fend off. Ma, Grandmother, and Auntie wielded it like a knife.

*I escaped for a half hour and kept my promise to Baba,* Asha thought defiantly, battling the power of the "eesh."

Inside the living room, the small cousins were hosting Reet at an otherwise all-doll tea party. Nobody else had gathered for real tea yet.

Asha handed the bowl of panthuas to Ma.

"What's this?" Ma asked.

"They're for you," Asha said. "From Baba."

The anger drained out of Ma's body. But Asha felt a twinge of guilt as she watched the veil drop across her mother's face again. Why had she reminded Ma of Baba's absence? Worst of all, the cousins gobbled up the round, juicy balls of sweet brown dough before Ma even had a chance to taste them. Now Asha was out of money *and* the regulation was explicit: A girl of Asha's age didn't venture out alone on the streets of Calcutta. Ever.

"Ma, come and see," Reet said quickly, getting up to crack the curtain. "They're out there again. Can you believe it? There's six of them now."

Ma hurried over. "There are?" She looked alert again, patting her hair into place distractedly. "Didi!" she called toward the kitchen. It was how she always addressed Auntie, even though the two of them weren't sisters. "Come quickly! You'll never believe what's happening outside."

As Auntie and the twins flanked Ma at the window, Reet backed away. "She asked where you were as soon as you left," Reet informed her sister. "I'm sorry, Osh. I had to tell her you went out."

"Oh well," Asha whispered back. "It was worth a try, anyway. I'll have to find a way to get some exercise inside the house."

"What about playing with them?" Reet asked, tilting her head toward the two little girls, who had lost interest in the scene outside the window. They were chattering and arranging their dolls in a congenial circle. "They're kind of overlooked sometimes, aren't they?"

*We all are, when you're around,* Asha thought. *At least by those idiots out there. Thank goodness.*

Ma widened the curtains a bit more. The onlookers outside were jostling each other for a better view of Reet drinking tea. Auntie and Ma giggled and whispered as they watched the watchers, but Asha blocked Reet as best as she could, standing with her back to the window.

"Tell us a Tuntuni story!" Sita commanded.

"Come beside me here," Asha said. "Reet's going to sing us a song while we do some yoga."

"I am?" Reet asked.

"She is?" Suma asked, looking a bit disappointed.

"Yes, she is. Sing that one about the two sisters, Reet. I haven't heard it in a while. The three of us are going to

44

stand in a row and do some exercises while we hear the song. I need to move around a bit." That, at least, was true.

· The three of them, stretching from side to side and swinging their arms in the air, left to right, right to left, must have blocked the view, because the crowd outside dispersed as Reet began the lighthearted Tagore song.

# SEVEN

THE POSTMAN ALWAYS LEFT THE MAIL AT THE GATE, AND ASHA took over the job of collecting it. One afternoon, she brought in an anonymous love note from one of Reet's admirers addressed "To the Beauty from Delhi."

As Reet read those words out loud, Asha caught her mother's arched eyebrows and open mouth. For a split second, she wondered if Ma thought the letter was intended for her, not her daughter. But nobody else noticed.

Baba sent two aerogrammes a week, covering every inch of blue paper with neatly printed Bangla words. It was strange how his handwriting in English was a scrawl, Asha thought, while his Bangla looked as if it could be in a book. He sent postcards to Asha and Reet with pictures of the Statue of Liberty standing in the harbor, the Empire State

Building, Wall Street, and other famous New York City landmarks. The few lines he scribbled on the backs of the cards were always in English, with a joke or two and a snippet of news.

He was sharing a flat with some other Bengali men who lived in a place called Flushing, Queens, he'd told the girls in the last one they'd received. No job yet, but he was starting to master the subway system as he went to interview after interview, mostly for lower-paying draftsman positions. He was studying hard to pass the professional engineering exam. If he did, he'd be more likely to get a high-paying job.

Grandmother always read Baba's aerogrammes first, even though they were clearly addressed to Ma, which infuriated Asha. She went to the roof to write out her frustration over this outright violation.

*What gives Grandmother the right to read somebody else's letters, S.K.? It must be the same law that lets Ma read my letters from Delhi. Kavita must know her letters are public documents. I've only received two, and they're short and boring. I've managed to write three myself, and kept them cheerful; Kavita's mother's not as old-fashioned as Ma, but you never know.*

The rainy season had finally started, and as slow, heavy drops began to fall, Asha curled tightly against the door, pulling herself and the diary under the small slanting tin roof that was the only shelter in sight.

*So Ma was right—our friendship is slipping away. The worst thing about her prophecies is that she has the power to make them come true. Well, at least I'm breaking a sweat these days—that helps me work off some of this stress.*

Thanks to her sister's suggestion, Asha had initiated a new cousin-based exercise plan. She taught Sita and Suma the basics of a good pillow fight, chasing them up and down the stairs while they giggled and squealed. She lay on her back with one cousin perched on her shins and lifted her feet up and down, fast, giving each a turn on the roller coaster of her body while they screamed and laughed. They played the Blind Bee game, with Asha tying a scarf across her eyes and buzzing while the twins circled her. Gingerly they tapped her and then ran away, singing out a rhyme that meant, "Hey, you buzzing bee! Sting us like you see!" Asha tried to grab them, chanting another rhyme: "I can't see, so don't blame me."

An hour later, she was sweaty, thirsty, and relaxed. The little girls kept asking for just one more game, though, so they played until either Auntie or Grandmother came upstairs to put an end to the fun.

"It's too much!" Asha overheard Grandmother complaining to Ma. "She gets the little ones so stirred up, they can't get a good night's sleep. How will they digest their dinners?"

Ma didn't answer, but, to Asha's surprise, Raj did. "The girls sleep like logs, Grandmother. And besides, they used to complain about going upstairs, remember? Now they're dragging Asha there as soon as dinner's over. The exercise is good for them."

Raj still hadn't said much of anything to Reet or Asha, but they'd finally noticed that he wasn't speaking to his parents much, either, and hardly teased his little sisters at all. Because it was so unusual for him to speak up these days, Asha felt even more warmed by his defense.

She and Reet talked about Raj's silence when the sisters were getting ready to join their sleeping cousins under the mosquito net. "Tell you what: Make the Boy Cuz talk and get a half-hour foot massage," Reet said, combing out her sister's hair.

"From him?" Asha asked, grinning.

"No, Your Royal Highness, from your one and only lady-in-waiting. Me."

Asha loved foot massages—she'd beg, whine, and wheedle until Reet caved in. Using baby oil, her sister would soften Asha's callused toes and cracked heels, finding just the right pressure points on the arches.

Asha's chance to rise to the challenge came one afternoon. She was reading "The Seven Swans" from *Grimms' Fairy Tales* aloud to the twins. Suma was perched cozily on Reet's lap, getting her hair braided, and Sita was leaning against Asha's shoulder, studying the illustrations. Ma and Auntie were giggling over the love note yet again, and Grandmother was rereading Baba's last letter.

Raj came inside early, swinging his cricket bat and mumbling under his breath. "What's wrong, Beta?" his mother asked, the tenderness in her voice making it clear that she was addressing her favorite child.

Asha stopped reading to peek at the twins. Did they notice the special treatment their brother always received—the finest piece of meat at dinner, his own room, access to their grandfather's chair in the living room? But Sita and Suma were waiting eagerly for the end of the story and weren't paying attention to their mother.

"Keep reading, Tuni Didi," they clamored, but she was listening to Raj.

"Not a soul on the cricket field," he was telling his mother. "And I really wanted to play."

Grandmother peered at Raj over her reading glasses. "You should be studying, like your friends. You'll be the head of this house one day, you know. Neither tennis nor cricket will put food on this table. Don't you realize that?"

"Yes, Grandmother, of course, Grandmother," Raj said, sounding like a tape recording.

Grandmother went back to Baba's letter. Baba's tone and words were always cheerful and optimistic, but Grandmother scrutinized them for any hint of his *real* condition. "Who is cooking for him?" she was muttering now. "Are they not hiring him because he's a foreigner?"

Raj slouched toward the stairs. They were just at the climax of "The Seven Swans," but Asha handed the book to her sister. "Finish it," she said.

None of the adults was paying any attention, and Sita moved closer to Reet to keep track of the story. Reet winked at Asha and immediately picked up where her sister had left off.

Asha grabbed Raj's bat from the corner of the room and

moved swiftly but quietly out to the stairwell before he could make his way up. "I'll bowl for you," she said, keeping her voice low. She used English, knowing that her cousin, too, spoke that language with his friends instead of Bangla.

Raj was surprised enough to look at her directly for once. "You? I thought you didn't play anymore, since..." His voice trailed off, and Asha finished the sentence in her mind: *you haf bee-come a voo-man.*

"I'm even better now. My friend and I used to practice in her garden." She flexed her arm, making the muscle bulge like a camel's hump.

Her cousin's eyes widened at the sight. "Come on, then." He was whispering now, too. "We can practice outside."

They stole past the cook, who had her back to the door, and entered the walled garden beside the house. Suddenly Ma's face peered out through the iron grating of a window. "Come inside right now, Tuni," she ordered.

Asha and Raj exchanged looks. "We're staying inside the garden, Auntie," Raj said, his voice and verb tenses dripping with courtesy. "Will you permit Tuni to bowl for me here, please? I really need the practice."

Ma frowned and began to move her head in the figure eight that meant no, no, no. Asha's heart sank. Her fingers were curving around a ball again, and she was longing to hurl it as fast and hard as she could.

"Oh, let them play inside the garden," came Grandmother's voice from behind Ma. "It won't do anybody any harm. And I don't know why you made such a fuss about her going down the street to buy a few sweets the other day. I'm sure none of the neighbors can even tell she's a grown woman."

No answer came from Ma, but she disappeared. Asha grinned as she took off her scarf and rolled up her sleeves. The one good thing about living in this house was that Grandmother could overrule Ma.

# EIGHT

THE SIDE GARDEN WAS NARROW BUT LONG, AND ASHA managed to give her cousin an hour of first-rate batting practice. She noticed right away that he was an excellent player, but she actually bowled a couple of bouncers, making his jaw drop.

After about an hour, Raj glanced up at their next-door neighbor's house. "Come and join us," he called.

Asha glimpsed the face in the fourth-story window, but again, it quickly disappeared. She frowned. It was disconcerting to be the object of attention; she'd guessed from her sister's constant audience that she herself would hate being ogled by strangers, and she'd been right. When someone you didn't know stared at you, it felt as if you were being robbed, the sight of you stolen with no intention of return.

"What's the real story with that neighbor?" she asked her cousin.

"Shhh . . . I'll tell you later. He'll hear us."

Asha didn't lower her voice. "He doesn't seem to care what we think or he wouldn't be spying. Why should I worry about his feelings?"

"Come inside, you two!" Auntie called. "The mosquitoes are swarming; it's almost evening."

"You *have* improved," Raj told Asha as they gathered their bats and the wicket. "You're as good as some of my friends. How's your tennis, by the way?"

"Better than my cricket," she said. It might not sound modest, but she was telling the truth. At least she hoped so—it had been months since she'd last held a racket. She felt a pang for the familiar grip of the lost Chris Evert in her hand.

"We'll have to play sometime," her cousin said. "We've got a tournament of sorts going at the college down the road, and we have some great matches. I'd love some extra practice before the next one."

She hesitated. "I can't, Raj. Ma won't let me play sports in public."

"We'll talk Grandmother into an override. Want me to try?"

Asha's heart leaped. To play tennis again, competing in the sun and open air against other good players, figuring out the perfect strategy to win a point . . . the temptation of it danced in her mind. She opened her mouth to accept her cousin's offer, but then remembered the promise she'd made Baba. *Take care of your mother, Tuni.* "No, Raj, don't. I can't have that happen to my mother. Baba wouldn't like it."

He shrugged. "Well, we can practice serves, tosses, and volleys in the garden, anyway. Hey—do you still play cards?"

"Baba and I play all the time."

"Really? Let's go."

She followed her cousin upstairs, feeling as if she'd been reinstated on the guest list at an exclusive club. His room was tidy, the way she remembered. Not many frills and not much clutter, just a couple of posters of tennis players and cricket stars, a blue and white cotton bedspread, white mosquito netting tied up overhead, a desk, and a shelf jammed with dusty books. Asha ran her index finger across the spines.

"Borrow them if you want," Raj told her. "I've killed them already."

Asha knew just what he meant. She'd already demolished the few books she'd brought along. They were dead, at least for a while. Certain stories could come back to life on the second, third, and even tenth reading if you gave them enough time between encounters. While she waited for her own favorites to recover, she was making her way through the books on her grandfather's shelf. But she missed the pleasure of a light read. Taking her time, she chose a handful of titles. Then she joined her cousin on the floor.

Raj was sitting cross-legged, shuffling the deck of cards again and again. She waited for him to deal them, but he didn't. Instead he placed the pile of cards on the floor and leaned back against the wall. From the expression on his face, Asha knew it was time to keep silent.

She waited.

"You're so lucky to be a girl," Raj blurted out finally.

She was so surprised by his words that she couldn't help responding. "What?"

"Girls don't have to become engineers, or doctors, or professors because '*those* jobs are so *prestigious*.' *You* can stay home and relax. You don't even have to go to school while you're here. They'd never let *me* get away with that."

He looked up, and Asha instinctively averted her gaze to focus on his hands, which were clenched.

"I'm—I'm a good cricket player, Osh." He punched both knees with his fists, hard enough to make Asha wince.

For the first time during this visit, he'd called Asha by name, and she knew it was time for her to speak. "You *are* good," she said, telling the truth. She'd learned from experience that truth was nonnegotiable for a secret keeper.

He leaned back again, sighed, and stretched out his legs. "But I have no chance to try and play for a living. Never. *You're the oldest son, Beta. You have to support the whole family someday, Beta.*" He looked away. "Sometimes I get so angry I can hardly speak."

A retort was whining in the back of Asha's mind: *You think YOU'VE got it hard? You don't know the first thing about life as a girl.* But that line of argument was suddenly silenced. Studying the angles of her cousin's cheek, she felt the bleakness of his future, the narrowness of his choices, the weight of responsibility he carried to provide for his grandmother, parents, sisters. "It's a heavy load," she said.

After another silence, Raj picked up the deck of cards again, and shuffled them a few times. "I'll teach you to play twenty-nine," he offered, his voice steady again. "You were too young to understand how trumps and bids worked last time."

"Baba already taught me. You need four players, though, don't you?"

He started dealing the cards. "We can practice with two."

"Sounds good. Raj, who is that strange person next door?"

"His name's Jay, but I don't know much more than that. When they moved in last summer, I went over to introduce myself—and to see if he was any good at cricket—but he hardly said a word."

"How old is he, then?"

"Twentyish. No friends. No sisters or brothers. Keeps to himself and mostly stays in his room."

"What does he do up there?"

"I don't know. Why are you so interested, anyway?"

"Oh, he stares over here a lot." She didn't add the words "at me," figuring her cousin would probably react in shocked disbelief. A man . . . staring at dark, skinny, flat-chested Asha Gupta? Besides, she didn't want anybody to find out that she'd been escaping up to the roof.

Raj shrugged. "Don't worry, he's harmless. Come on, Tuni, let's play a hand or two and challenge my parents after dinner. They're undefeated in the neighborhood, but it would be so fabulous if we beat them."

After she and Raj had been soundly trounced by Auntie

and Uncle in a couple of games of twenty-nine and the little girls had enjoyed a good long romp, Asha lit a candle and propped her feet in her sister's lap. The small cousins were already asleep, nestled against each other like a pair of spoons.

"You win," Reet said, pouring baby oil into her palm. "Raj talked to us both nonstop at dinner *and* during the card game. How'd you break the spell, you sorceress?"

"It's called the magic of sports, Reet." *And the power of secrets,* she thought. "Focus on the arches, will you?"

# NINE

THE NEIGHBORHOOD'S INTEREST IN REET DIDN'T SEEM TO BE waning. Every afternoon, ignoring the mud in the lane and the rain falling on their umbrellas, admirers gathered near the gate. They stayed there until Uncle stalked out grimly to put on the big padlock, signifying that the household was closing down for the night.

Grandmother pushed past Ma and Auntie to shut the curtains firmly, but that didn't prevent Reet's fan club from tossing flowers through the bars onto the path. Or singing love songs at the tops of their not-so-tuneful voices.

"Fools, all of them," Grandmother said, and Asha heartily agreed.

Her own watcher's interest wasn't abating, either. She fumed in her corner of the roof as he gazed at her from across the way. *I'm not budging, S.K.,* she told her diary. *I'm NOT losing the only place I can be alone because Some Monk is obsessed with watching me write.*

As for Ma, the brief thrill of her older daughter's debut in the neighborhood was soon subdued once again by the pressure of living under a roof that wasn't her own. She was getting quiet again, and the girls knew exactly who was closing in for the kill. In desperation, Reet proposed a jaunt of pleasure shopping. "Puja season starts in a couple of months," she said, ignoring Grandmother's frown.

"I suppose you're right," Ma said hesitantly. "You girls must have some decent festival clothes to wear if your father . . ." *. . . doesn't send for us by then.* Asha finished her mother's sentence in her head, her stomach twisting. It had been almost four months since Baba had left for America. Had he passed that engineering test? How much longer would they have to wait?

"And how will you afford such a purchase?" Grandmother asked.

"Bintu left us enough money for *clothes,*" Ma said haughtily. "He likes to see me and his daughters looking nice."

Grandmother sniffed but didn't pursue her interrogation, and they took her silence as permission. Raj rounded up two cycle rickshaws and brought them to the gate. Auntie and Ma took Sita and Suma with them, and Raj, Reet, and Asha squished into the other.

Asha wished fervently but uselessly that she could stay home with Grandmother. War refugees blanketed the pavements, and too-skinny children made Asha's heart ache with helpless pity. But if she had to be honest, even more than interacting with destitute children, she hated the thought of trying on clothes in front of so many critical eyes.

Her sister's admirers were already gathering as the family departed. They goggled at Reet as she eased herself into the rickshaw, then looked disappointed as they drove away, like ticket holders who'd just been told the performance had been canceled.

"Shoo, why don't you," Raj said as the rickshaw passed the young men. But his tone was flat and hopeless.

The wiry rickshaw pullers had to stand on the pedals, lugging the Gupta daughters-in-law and their offspring from the southern outskirts of the city to the main shopping center in Gariahat Corner. Beggars crowded around the women as soon as they climbed onto the sidewalk. Raj escaped the outstretched hands and whining voices by ducking into a bookseller. Asha was about to follow him when she saw Ma beckoning furiously from the front of a saree shop. Sighing, Asha turned from the lure of the books and trudged over to her mother and sister. Auntie and the cousins were already trooping inside.

A clerk greeted them, his excitement at welcoming a pair of suburban housewives shaping itself into an expansive grin. "How might I serve you ladies?" he asked, rubbing his palms together.

"Sarees for festival season," Ma announced. "Silk only, please."

Ma pushed Asha forward, and the clerk began trying a series of different silks against her skin.

"Stand still, Tuni," Ma said sternly, once she and Asha were behind the curtain in the small alcove.

Reluctantly Asha obeyed, putting up one arm, then the next so Ma could tuck and fold the long piece of cloth around her. Locked in her one-armed pose while Ma pleated the front of the saree, she was reminded of the card Baba had sent with the picture of a statue standing in New York's harbor. "I look like the Statue of Liberty, Reet," Asha called through the curtain. "Isn't she wearing a saree, too?"

Ma sighed. "I suppose we'll take the mustard-colored one. It's the only one that suits your complexion." She pulled open the curtain.

Asha didn't bother looking in the mirror; she could tell how she looked by the expressionless faces before her. Reet was smiling, though, so Asha straightened and put up one arm again to hold an imaginary torch.

"Go stand in the Atlantic right now," her sister ordered, and they laughed.

Auntie ignored this sisterly exchange. "Too bad Tuni got your husband's dark complexion," she said, shaking her head in that annoying figure eight. "And she's all muscle, too, built like a boy. Quite the opposite of you, Sumitra. And our lovely Shona, of course."

Asha closed her lips tightly. She couldn't take any more of this "dark" stuff. What did a person's skin color have to do with *anything*? Especially beauty, of all things. An angry lecture was taking shape in her mind, and she was just about to spew it out when, behind her, the "lovely Shona" began to hum.

"My turn!" Reet said brightly. "Osh, why don't you go

and find Raj? He'll have to round up some rickshaws soon, won't he, Ma?"

"Take the parcel with you after the clerk wraps your saree, Tuni," Ma commanded, taking a gold-embroidered saree and Reet into the curtained alcove.

Auntie nodded and the twins squealed in delight when Ma pulled open the curtains this time.

"She's perfect," Auntie said. "Absolutely gorgeous."

"Shonadi, you look like a film star!" Sita cried.

"Yes, your younger sister is looking quite nice in that one, madam," the clerk told Ma, handing Asha the bulky parcel that was her new saree. The cousins giggled. Auntie quickly set the clerk straight, but Ma was already pulling open her bag to buy the magic saree.

# TEN

Most of the neighborhood was resting with the cur-tains closed against the heat. When the rains held back for a day or two, the earth steamed like a panful of rice. Asha was alone on the roof, writing furiously, drops of sweat smearing the words on the page. Jay the Hermit was spying on her through the slats of the shutters, but for once she didn't care. She had to write, she had to be alone, she could hardly believe what was happening.

Inside the house, the servants, Ma, and Auntie weren't napping as they usually did. They were preparing the house for the arrival of a guest so important that Uncle was com-ing home early. The house sparkled with an extra measure of polish, and Grandmother had splurged on some special sweets from the corner shop.

Asha could hear the twins waking from their nap and clattering downstairs to play hopscotch on the front path. They didn't know that this was an unusual day—the first time a girl in their generation would receive a wedding proposal, a herald of changes to come.

Uncle had received a message from another man in the neighborhood. Apparently this fellow had a nephew who was so besotted with Reet's charms that he could no longer wait to secure her as his. A formal proposal would take place today over tea, with the two older men meeting for a private discussion.

*Oh, S.K., if only my sister weren't so gorgeous. It's always getting her in trouble, and now the worst has happened. At first I thought the whole thing was a joke, but now I'm not so sure. Ma was eighteen when she married Baba, and Auntie was seventeen, Reet's age, when she married Uncle. He was twenty-six or so, just like Reet's Lusting Idiot.*

*I'm NEVER letting them marry my sister off. Especially not to someone who proposes without knowing anything about her except what she looks like. In America, girls our age are standing up for their rights, marching in protests, changing the world. But Reet and I aren't in America. Not yet, anyway. Come on, Baba, COME ON!*

*Maybe Uncle's just going through the motions for courtesy's sake. But why doesn't Reet tell him straightaway that she has NO desire to get married? She's already calling this suitor Y.L.I. for "Young Lusting Idiot" when the two of us are alone. So why doesn't she speak up for herself?*

*But I know the answer to that question, don't I? Her lack of protest, as usual, is for our mother's sake. The Jailor loosened the chains when the attention first started, but that didn't last long; now he seems to have retreated quite a bit. Ma talked a mile a minute yesterday and this morning, bragging to Auntie and Grandmother that she herself had received twelve proposals before the age of twenty. I wanted to scream. She'd never bothered to tell Reet and me that particular detail about her past. Is that some fantastic accomplishment? I don't think so. Anyway, I'm sure Uncle isn't taking this seriously. At least I hope not. But if he IS trying to marry my sister off, he'll have to deal with ME first.*

The pencil snapped in half because she was clutching it so tightly. Suddenly she slammed her diary shut, stood up, and twisted like a cobra about to spring.

"What are you staring at?" she demanded of the shutters across the way.

To her surprise they flew open, and so did the window behind them. Their neighbor leaned out. "What are you writing?" he retorted.

"None of your business," Asha answered, checking quickly to make sure the coconut trees barricaded them from sight. If anybody saw them talking, her reputation in the neighborhood would probably be tarnished forever. *Not that I care,* she thought, noticing for the first time that her watcher's hair was longer than that of most young men his age. He was wearing only an undershirt, and she felt a twinge of irritation that his arms were more muscular than any recluse deserved. "I *don't* like to be spied on," she added with a scowl, folding her arms across her chest.

"I haven't been spying on you," he said. "I've been studying you."

That made her even madder. "Oh. Studying. And just how is that different than spying?"

He swallowed, hesitated, and took a deep breath. "I want to— I'd like to . . . paint a portrait. Of you." The last five words came hurtling out of him like arrows, making her feel even more like a bull's-eye.

"Well, you can't," she said. "How dare you paint me without asking my permission?"

"I haven't started yet. I have been sketching, though, and trying to gather the courage to ask."

"Well, I don't give it to you." She turned to go.

"Wait!" he called. "I'm not a beginner, if that's what you're worried about. I studied art in Moscow for a year. A couple of gallery owners in Delhi and Leningrad who like my landscapes have been wanting me to try a portrait, but I haven't found anybody I want to paint. That is, until now."

"So that's why you've been spying on me. Well, I don't want anyone watching me or anybody in my family; I don't care if it's for the greatest masterpiece on the planet."

"Oh, I see. You're angry about the rabble on the corner.

Listen, I'm sorry on behalf of my sex, but I haven't joined in their pastime, in case you hadn't noticed. I've got better things to do."

"Like what?"

"Like this."

A paper bird soared over the space between their houses and landed at Asha's feet. She wanted to stomp on it, but somehow she couldn't. She didn't bend to pick up his gift, though, and neither she nor the painter spoke for a few moments.

"Let me paint you, Osh," he said finally, breaking the silence. "Please?"

She ignored the question. "You know my *nickname*? What else have you discovered about me?"

"I'm sorry. Our houses are so close, and your sister calls your name when she wants you. Don't tell me you haven't found out everything you can about me. But that's okay, it's going to help the painting to learn as much as we can about each other. By the way, my name's Jay Sen."

"I'm absolutely not interested in finding out anything more about you," Asha said, wondering why she didn't just leave. But something in his face was making her stay, and she could sense that he was telling the truth—a practice she always appreciated.

"Just think about it before you say no," he said. "Take the sketch. Look at it. Give us a chance, Osh. Please. Give our painting a chance."

She groaned. *He's not shy,* she realized. *Just odd. And persistent. But harmless probably, like Raj said.*

Downstairs, Uncle's voice was calling out a hearty welcome to his guest. It was time for the proposal. Picking up the paper bird, Asha quickly tucked it into her diary and left the roof without another word. She wanted to be sure she was in place in time to eavesdrop.

# ELEVEN

Asha crept down and perched on the hall stairs beside her sister, who was already sitting there. Raj emerged from his room and joined them. Only Uncle was in the living room; Grandmother, Auntie, and Ma were in the kitchen, and the twins had been sent next door to play with a friend. Auntie occasionally bustled out to refill the teacups or add biscuits to the platter of goodies. She was too distracted by the momentous occasion to look up and spot the three extra listeners.

The Lusting Idiot's uncle got to the point almost immediately. "Your two nieces have been staying under this roof for quite some time now. I've heard the older one is a lovely girl. Might she be interested in considering my nephew's proposal, as we discussed yesterday?"

Uncle didn't hesitate. "My nieces and their mother are

transferring residence to New York," he said importantly. "The president of the United States recently opened the door to Indian professionals, haven't you heard? My brother is there now, securing a job."

*He has a right to be proud,* Asha thought, wanting to applaud her uncle's reply. Baba was one of the first in the neighborhood to go to New York.

Uncle's guest raised the stakes. "Your brother's been gone for some time already. When will he send for his wife and daughters?"

A pause. "Soon."

Another pause. "What a generous man you are," their visitor said, his words slathered with sarcasm. "If he doesn't find work, you'll have to support your nieces indefinitely. I hear he tried to find something here in Calcutta. No luck, eh?"

On the steps, Reet caught Asha's shirt collar in the nick of time. Asha muttered a forbidden swearword under her breath, but subsided when Reet didn't let go.

"So many strikes and protests," Uncle was saying. "Businesses shutting down. No money to build new roads and bridges. Tough times for our engineers these days. Mrs. Gandhi is holding on, though. She'll turn us around."

"Some engineers haven't felt the pinch," retorted the other man smugly. "My brother, for example, just built a new house with a private flat attached where his son will live after he gets married. He's the only son in the family, and we have to prepare for his future, as you know yourself. That's why we want to secure a lovely girl from a good family."

"Who does he think he is?" Asha muttered, gripping the banisters so tightly it felt as if her knuckles were going to explode through her skin. "Why doesn't Uncle tell him to prepare his nephew's boring future far away from us?"

"I know his nephew," Raj whispered, as though the identity of the Y.L.I. had just dawned on him. "None of us can stand him."

"Shh-hhh," Reet said softly. "I want to listen."

"We're prepared for the fact that your niece will bring little or no dowry," said their guest. "How many suitors will accept that?"

"My niece has a perfectly adequate dowry," Uncle answered haughtily. "But in a few weeks' time, if my nieces are still with us, I shall contact you about this matter. I want only the best for my brother's children; I love them like my own. Perhaps arranging a good match is one service I can do for him."

Asha couldn't believe what she'd heard. What was Uncle saying? He wasn't rejecting the proposal, he was *postponing* it. Raj snorted in disgust and got up without meeting his cousins' eyes. They heard his door close with a sharp click.

Asha reached for Reet's hand. It was cold; her sister's face looked strangely vacant. "Don't worry," Asha whispered. "We're leaving for America soon, remember?"

But were they? They had no idea when Baba would send for them. It could take him weeks, months, or even a year to find a job. As long as they were living under this roof, Uncle could make any arrangements he wanted for his nieces. He might think he was doing Baba a favor by securing Reet a rich husband. Baba, in turn, might not be able to do anything once his older brother started negotiations. Especially if Ma didn't object. Or Reet herself.

"Let's go," Asha whispered. "We've heard enough."

The girls went upstairs and pulled the curtain to their room closed. They sat on the bed and looked at each other.

"Why don't you say something?" Asha asked. "Tell them you don't want to get married. They'll listen to you."

"They might. They might not. Besides, Ma seems to think it's a good idea."

"Think of yourself for once, Reet," Asha said. "This isn't a saree or a hairstyle you're letting her pick; it's a husband. For life."

"I'll say something before it's too late. For now, Ma seems so happy I don't want to ruin it for her."

"Once these things get started, how do you stop them? What if you can't?"

"I don't know. I'm hoping Baba will send for us and that will put an end to it. Could you believe how prideful that man sounded?"

"Disgusting. If his nephew's anything like that, you'd better storm down there right now and tell them you're not in the least bit interested."

"That's what you would do," Reet said, a bit wistfully.

"I'll do it for you."

"No. I can handle it. You'd just get in trouble. Besides, Baba's telegram is coming any day now."

The twins had returned and burst into the room. "Come on, Tuni Didi," they said. "Time for a game."

Asha got up. "Let me know if you want me to do

anything," she said, leaving Reet leaning against the wall, hands clasped so tightly in her lap, it looked as if she were praying.

"I'll be down in a minute," Asha told the twins as she paused by Raj's door.

She knocked.

"Who is it?" Raj called, clearly irritated.

"Me."

"Oh. Come in."

Asha closed the door once she was inside his room. "Tell me what you know about this fellow," she said.

"He's a good tennis player but a terrible sport. I know him through our tournaments on Friday afternoons. He's always trying to bend the rules to make things go his way."

"You've got rules? I thought it was just show up and play."

"Oh no. It's fairly strict. You've got to wear white shorts, a cap, and a collared shirt, and you need to bring along some decent tennis balls and a one-rupee note. About fifteen or twenty of us usually show up, and boys come from neighborhoods all around the southern part of the city. Losers are eliminated in best-of-seven-game matches until the two best players meet in a final match. The winner of that match takes the week's prize money home. Your sister's lover wins most of the time; he's one of those gloating types who try to make the rest of us feel bad. *And* he tries to stack the matches so he always faces the worst players."

"Tunidi, come on!" the girls were clamoring from downstairs.

"Off to be a blind bee again," she told Raj.

"Better you than me."

# TWELVE

Asha opened Jay's paper bird late that night, after her cousins and sister were asleep. In the candlelight, the sketch glowed as though it were already painted. In it, Asha was bent over her diary, scribbling as if her life depended on it. Wisps of loose hair made the viewer feel the wind blowing through them. Behind her, the coconut tree bowed low like a protector. A storm was coming, but the girl in the sketch didn't notice the clouds on the horizon. She was writing, but something in the curve of her shoulders and the tilt of her head made Asha's heart ache. The girl in the sketch seemed so vulnerable. And alone. Was that how Asha seemed to Jay in real life?

Jay was good, there was no doubt about that. Just from this quick sketch she could tell that a finished painting would be beautiful. If only the subject he was portraying didn't seem so powerless. Why had he drawn her like that?

The next afternoon, she took the sketch to the rooftop and waited. After a few minutes, his shutters opened and he leaned out, smiling as he saw the unfolded bird in her hand. "What did you think?"

"It's good," she said. "But it doesn't look like me."

"Why not?"

"The girl in your drawing seems . . . oh, I don't know, so much younger and weaker than I am. Plus she's stupid. A storm's coming and there she is, still sitting outside. She could at least have taken cover under the shelter."

"I didn't set out to make you look weak. I drew it as it came to me."

A voice in the back of her head was telling her to shut up, but for once she didn't listen to it. "Did you know I'm a champion tennis player? And that I scored the highest marks in my class ten years in a row?"

"No, but—"

"Did you know I can throw a cricket ball as hard as any boy in this town?"

"I've seen you play, but—"

"You're obviously completely mistaken about me." Why was she so angry? And she'd never bragged about her accomplishments before; she used to get embarrassed when Baba boasted about them at dinner parties. Now she was doing it herself, and to this odd stranger. What was *wrong* with her?

"Give me a chance to fix it, Osh. Let me paint you. The *real* you. Smart, powerful, strong. I can do it, I promise."

Asha was quiet. What could it hurt to let him paint her? She came up there every day anyway, and she'd been enduring his staring for weeks now. "Oh, all right. Do what you need to do. Just don't ever tell my mother we had this conversation. Or spoke at all. I'm already walking a thin line."

"Quite a thin line I'm walking over here, too," he said. "My mother's the kindest woman on the planet, so she doesn't scold or nag much. She does, however, sacrifice so many flowers before the gods and goddesses for my sake that her prayer room's turned into a botanical garden."

Asha had to smile; Grandmother's prayer room was also well stocked with flowers and fruit in honor of Baba's job quest. "They don't want you to paint, do they?"

"They think I'm insane. But it's something I have to do. Something I was born to do. Can you understand that?"

She nodded. "I have a dream too," she said slowly.

"You do?"

"Yes."

He didn't say anything, and she recognized the attentive silence she herself offered when someone was about to confess something important.

The truth came pouring out before she could stop it: "I want to be a psychologist."

"I've heard of that, but tell me more."

"It's a mender of the mind. Someone who helps people release their secrets so they can be free." She laughed, amazed that she'd told him more than she'd even told Reet. "Doesn't that sound like I need a mind healer myself?"

"You'll be perfect," he said. "A confidante for those in trouble."

Asha shrugged, refolded the sketch, and flew it back to him. "All right. Paint away. Make sure this time she looks like me."

He caught and crushed the paper in his fist. "I'll do my best. You won't even know I'm here."

"I'm not going to wear the same clothes every day," she warned.

"You don't have to. I'm going to paint you in the green salwar you wore the first afternoon you arrived. The one with the white flowers embroidered on the hem and sleeves."

He was talking about her traveling salwar, the one that she loved because Baba had picked it out.

"And I'm not going to wear shoes," she added. "I like being barefoot."

"You don't have to. Your feet are beautiful; they were one of the first things I noticed about you. I love your high arches and the ankle bracelets you sometimes wear."

Reet insisted on Asha's wearing the bracelets when she dressed up, and she'd grown to like the jangle of them herself. But why were her cheeks so hot? Was it because this was the first time anybody had used the word "beautiful" when talking about her?

*Settle down, he's talking about your feet, not you. But still.* "My hair gets messy in the wind," she said before she could stop herself. "I don't always keep it in a braid."

"I like it loose. It glows in the sunlight like silk. In fact, I'm going to paint it like that."

The double thumps were becoming more regular; now, each time Jay spoke, her heart pounded out an extra beat.

"Osh, time for tea!" It was Reet.

Asha and Jay smiled at each other one last time across the gap, before Asha turned to go. Suddenly she was conscious of the swing of her long braid behind her, the way her feet landed as she took each step, and the melody of ankle bracelets accompanying her like dance music as she left the roof.

# THIRTEEN

Asha came up with two plans to keep her sister safe from the Y.L.I. She wasn't happy about either of them, but they were all she had. Plan A: Confront the family, which required just the right timing.

"The astrologer said they're a good match," Uncle said as the elders in the family discussed the proposal one afternoon.

"He's an only son *and* the eldest grandson," Auntie added. "I don't know if you'll find any situation better than that."

"Like you," Asha muttered to Raj in the corner where the two of them were drinking their tea. "That means *you'll* get your pick of girls, too. Just like the Idiot."

Raj frowned. "I would never pick a girl because of the way she looks through a pair of binoculars. I can't stand this." He put his cup down and stalked outside with his cricket bat as though he wanted to bash someone over the head with it.

Reet sat next to Ma, listening to her future being discussed as though she herself wasn't even in the room. Uncle, Grandmother, and Auntie reviewed the suitor's wealth, status, behavior, education, career potential, and child-rearing capacity. The fact that he was still a student weighed against him; he should be established in his career before venturing into marriage. But Reet would be well taken care of; the boy's family was one of the richest in town; the stars were aligned in the right places.

"Should we accept this proposal?" Uncle asked once they'd finished their full evaluation.

"Yes," said Grandmother.

"Yes," said Auntie.

Ma kept silent, and so did Reet.

Asha took a deep breath. It was time to implement Plan A.

She stood behind her sister and placed her hands on Reet's shoulders, announcing in a strong, loud voice: "Reet doesn't want to get married. So you'll have to say no to this ridiculous proposal."

The conversation screeched to a halt. Reet's shoulders tensed under Asha's fingers. Three pairs of disapproving adult eyes immediately focused on Ma.

Across the table, Ma's expression flickered and then faded, reminding Asha of how the small television screen at Kavita's house sometimes lost reception.

"These girls were given entirely too much freedom in

Delhi," Uncle said, swiveling his head in that horrible figure eight. "They don't know how to behave properly."

*Too much freedom?* Asha thought. *Hah!* "She doesn't want to get married," she said again, trying to muster as much confidence in her voice as she had the first time. "Right, Reet?"

Nobody spoke or moved, except for Uncle, whose head was still dancing with disapproval.

"I trust my elders to make the right decision," Reet said, but her voice was flat.

The atmosphere lightened; the conversation resumed. Uncle launched into yet another description of the new flat and expensive furniture that Lusting Idiot and wife would receive as wedding gifts from his parents.

Reet half turned in her chair so that nobody else could see her face. "Sorry, Osh," she mouthed, and her eyes flicked over to their mother. "Can't do that to her."

Asha sighed. "No worries," she whispered, bending to kiss her sister on the cheek.

She went upstairs and pulled a brown paper bag out from under their bed. Carrying it up to the roof, she left it in the shelter of the small tin overhang and walked to the wall. It was about to rain again, and neighbors were beginning to close windows and yank laundry off the lines. Down on the cricket pitch, her cousin wasn't even bothering to break into his buddies' game.

Asha was glad that the darkening sky was starting to make people scurry inside. There was something heartening about seeing others dash for cover when you were about to brave a storm. It made you feel ready to take a risk, even willing to try something crazy. And that was good, because it was time for Plan B—and Plan B was absolutely insane.

Asha desperately needed to hash it over with someone before she set things in motion. How she wished Kavita were here! Not only would Kavita listen to Asha's ideas, she'd add details and anticipate trouble spots. But Kavita was far away in Delhi; Asha hadn't heard from her friend in weeks. She thought for a moment of finding Raj and telling him what she was about to do, but she didn't want him *or* Reet to bear any of the consequences. She'd do the deed; she'd take the punishment. Still, it would be wonderful to talk the plan through with another human being.

Asha turned around to study the shutters shielding Jay's room. Where was he, anyway? Usually, five minutes or so after she came out to the roof, his window would fly open and the two of them would start talking. But there was no sign of her neighbor across the way.

Monsoon clouds, dark and heavy, drew closer to each other. Crows screeched warnings from the coconut trees as the wind began to pick up. "Tuni!" Ma shouted from below. "Where *is* that girl? Does anybody know?"

"She's upstairs, Ma," Reet's voice answered. "Probably resting."

Windows banged as Ma and Auntie hurried to storm-proof the house. The boys on the field called their cricket game and dispersed. Rain was starting to fall; slow, steaming drops that hissed as they landed. Asha watched a pattern of dark gray spread across the lighter dry expanse of roof.

Raj, heading into the house through the side yard,

looked up, glimpsed his cousin, and grinned. Asha basked in the affection she saw in his face; she'd worked hard to earn it. Sadly, though, that smile was probably the last he'd give her for a while, because the first step in Plan B involved robbing him. She was going to have to borrow a racket, balls, one rupee, and a pair of shorts, a shirt, and a cap in order for the plan to work.

The goal of the plan was to make sure the Y.L.I. never wanted to see Reet again; Asha was going to have to shame him so that he slunk away with his head down. What was the best way to put a boy like that in his place? A girl had to beat him soundly, as the American player Billie Jean King had humiliated her nemesis, Bobby Riggs. Three straight sets in front of all those watching eyes.

Asha knew Plan B had lots of pitfalls; maybe she should discard it altogether. Even the weather might not cooperate— Raj had been grumbling about the storms that had been drenching the tennis courts on Friday afternoons. Her cousin might catch her borrowing his things. The getaway part was even trickier. How would she sneak out of the house without anybody seeing? Even if she did manage to escape, the college boys might guess that she was a girl *before* she got to win the tournament. And what if she couldn't even remember how to hit the ball over the net?

She stood up and began pacing the roof. "The name's Gupta," she said, trying to make the pitch of her voice sound less like a girl. That was all she'd have to announce to the boys who organized the tournament, and thankfully it was a common enough name. Her voice squeaked the first two times she practiced it. Lightning flashed, followed by the deep rumble of thunder. Asha tried to imitate it: "The name's Gupta. Boom!"

The storm was intensifying, so she ducked back under the angled sheet of rippled tin. She'd come to the hardest part of her plan, the step that would set things in motion. Bringing her braid in front of her shoulder, she stroked its length. Her sister combed Asha's hair out every night before bed, humming or singing while she eased out the tangles. Then Reet wove it into a single thick, heavy braid. It was so long now that Asha had to move it out of the way before she sat down. How had Jay described it? "Glowing in the sunlight like silk."

It was no use; she had to save Reet. She had to do what came next.

Opening the paper bag, Asha pulled out a pair of sharp kitchen shears, closed her eyes for a moment, and pictured her sister's face. Then she held up her long, wet braid. Quickly, before she could change her mind, she sliced it off as close to the nape of her neck as she could manage. Snap! The braid dangled like a heavy rope from her hand, and she glanced again at Jay's closed window.

She wound the orphaned hair into a flat, tight coronet, took a few pins out of the bag, and pinned the spiral back into place. Hopefully, she'd avoid Reet's nightly brush, and nobody would be able to tell that her braid was no longer attached to her scalp until after she'd carried out her plan.

# FOURTEEN

ASHA KNEW THAT FOR PLAN B TO HAVE EVEN A FAINT HOPE OF succeeding, she'd need a bunch of miracles. To her amazement, they came.

Miracle Number One: It didn't rain the next day. The sun blazed down, drying the dirt roads by early afternoon, which was when Asha started getting ready.

Miracle Number Two: Raj's clothes fit her perfectly. She wrapped a white cotton towel snugly around her torso before putting on his shorts, and it hid everything. *Good thing I'm as flat as a chapatti bread,* she thought. She'd been secretly wondering how Jay was going to paint certain parts of her body in the portrait he was working on. Would he wish she was built more like Reet? For now, she pushed all those thoughts out of her mind. Plan B first; then her daydreaming could drift back to other subjects.

Her reflection in her cousin's mirror looked exactly like a skinny first-year college boy. She swallowed when she saw her bony knees—she knew exactly what Ma and Auntie would say about *a good Bengali girl showing the world her legs.* Ma had gotten rid of Asha's shorts and pants after *that* day and filled her closet with frocks and salwars, most of them hand-me-downs from Reet. But Indian boys wore shorts when they played sports, so today Asha was going to have to expose a bit of thigh in public.

Miracle Number Three: She was able to tiptoe out of the house without anybody in the family seeing her. Grandmother and Auntie were busy in the kitchen. Raj had already left for the tennis courts. Ma was nowhere in sight, and the small cousins were in the living room playing with Reet.

Asha stopped first in the side yard at the pile of garbage waiting to be burned. Using the sweeper's fire-stoking stick, she shoved her braid deep into the middle of the pile. *Sorry, Jay,* she thought with a pang. *You were right; it was beautiful. You're going to have to imagine it to finish the rest of your painting.*

By now, Asha could close the front gate without making a sound. She rounded a corner and started down the narrow dirt path that circled the pond and led to the college. The grip of Raj's extra racket felt good in her hand. Even though it was old, the wood wasn't warped and the strings were tight. She tried not to notice how unfamiliar the sunlight and air felt against her thighs and how light her skull felt without the weight of her hair. A herd of cows stared with mournful, hungry eyes, and Asha fought the impulse to cover her legs.

A dozen naked little boys splashed in the pond, wet skin gleaming like polished wood. Their mothers kept a close eye on them, chatting, washing sarees, scrubbing copper pots. None of them noticed Asha, nobody turned to gawk, and she felt a bit more confident in her disguise.

The college was just beyond the row of tiny shacks where the neighborhood's servants lived. The campus was small, but Asha noticed that the cricket pitch was in perfect shape. She took a deep breath and walked toward the group of boys gathered beside the four clay courts. Again, nobody paid any attention at all, and she easily placed Raj's rupee in the empty tennis ball can and joined the queue waiting to sign up for the tournament.

"Gupta's the name," her voice grunted perfectly. Miracle Number Four.

But then the unexpected happened: Raj, who was practicing on one of the courts, recognized her. He tripped, regained his balance, and let his racket slip out of his hand. Asha hadn't taken her cousin's reaction into consideration. Would he wreck the whole thing?

Raj bent down to pick up his racket. Then, to Asha's amazement, he turned away and went back to rallying with his opponent as though nothing had happened. Oh, he was wonderful! Somehow she managed not to race across the court and hug him, thereby ruining the whole plan herself. Instead she vowed to repay him with hours of cricket practice. *Miracle Number Five,* she thought.

Now how was she going to hit? Baba had taught her strategies to defeat every kind of player, and she was naturally consistent. She'd been at the top of her game before Ma had made her quit playing at the club. After that, she and Kavita had practiced in the garden every chance they could, but it had been a while since she'd held a racket in her hand. During the warm-up, Asha was relieved to see her skills returning and her shot placement growing more accurate.

The rules were to play seven games, with the first player who won four moving to the next round. Asha's first opponent was a chubby boy who was panting heavily by the second point. She dropped one game out of sheer nervousness, sending double faults into the net as though she were a beginner. Score: 4-1. *No more unforced errors,* she told herself sternly as they shook hands at the net.

In her second match, Asha played a dim-witted fellow who hardly understood the basics of the game. It was quick work, and she started to feel the old thrill of placing a shot perfectly, or racing after—and smashing—a high ball that seemed impossible to reach. Score: 4-0.

Third round, she was pitted against a fairly decent player who got nervous under pressure and lost the big points. Asha had settled into her game by now, and she wasn't missing her slice shots or volleys. Score: 4-1.

After only an hour, she reached the fourth round. There she discovered with some concern that she was about to face Raj. The desire not to crush her cousin was short-lived as her competitive spirit asserted itself, and she settled into the rhythm of their long rallies with gusto. Raj was good, but she was better. She won 4-3, but this match took about as long as the other three matches put together.

Raj raised his eyebrows when they shook hands at the net. "Nice shorts," he whispered. Asha's cheeks felt ten degrees hotter, but she grinned and nodded.

Finally it was time to face her target—the Y.L.I. He had demolished his opponents even faster than she had and had been watching her play against Raj. She'd had no chance to watch his game and spot weaknesses, but he'd obviously been taking note of hers.

Asha checked him out from head to toe while he spun his racket. She had to admit he was handsome, but his expression was smug, full of confidence that he could get what he wanted, do what he wanted, be what he wanted. How dare he think he could get her sister just because he desired her? Asha had never hated anyone more in her life.

"Up or down?" he asked, getting ready to spin his racket.

"Down," Asha said, keeping her voice deep.

"It's up," he said.

Asha fought a wave of fear as her opponent served the first point, but the fear disappeared quickly. Miracle Number Six: The Y.L.I. was a serve-and-volley man who couldn't handle lobs and passing shots. They got to deuce several times, but he didn't manage to win even a single game. He was quivering with rage by the last point, which she ended by placing a gorgeous, spinning lob just out of his reach.

Furious, the Y.L.I. stalked to the net for the required handshake, and Asha trotted up to join him. Just before their hands met, she whipped off Raj's cap and gave her head a good shake. What was left of her hair—now chin-length—came tumbling down.

"Your uncle spoke with *my* uncle a while back," she told him, using her normal voice. *A girly voice,* she'd always complained to Reet. *It's got no ooomph to it.* Now, however, she felt immensely powerful as she used it to make a public declaration: "My sister's not interested in your offer. Thanks, but no thanks."

He pulled his hand out of her grip as though it were on fire and backed away.

"That's not a boy!" Asha heard the other players shout. "It's your cousin, Raj! It's that girl from Delhi! The younger one!" And then: "Look! She's wearing shorts!"

Asha strode off the court without looking back, the jeers and hoots and catcalls fading behind her. Out of the corner of her eye, she noticed the Y.L.I. disappearing fast in the other direction. Head down, just as she'd intended.

Raj caught up with her at the cricket pitch. "You weren't lying about your game," he said. "You're good. Really good."

Asha was surprised by how relieved she felt. Raj was grinning; he wasn't mad. She handed him the racket she was carrying and tucked her hair back under the cap. "Sorry for the shock. And thanks for the racket, by the way."

"No problem," he said. "But you should have told me what you were up to. I'd have loaned you my good racket. Anything to put that fool in his place. Oh, and here's your prize money. They took a vote and decided to give it to you." He held out a tennis ball can stuffed with rupees.

Asha didn't take it. "Keep it. It's rent for your clothes and racket, plus I nicked a rupee from your desk drawer."

"No," he said. "You earned it."

She shook her head. "I can't go out to spend it."

"I insist."

She took the can and counted out a few rupees and handed back the can. "I'll keep some for beggars. Buy my ma sweets, though, will you? And then get a new cricket magazine or two. We'll both read them."

Raj shrugged, slipped the rest of the money into his pocket, and tossed the empty can to a shirtless boy, who caught it with delight.

"They'll find out at home, you know," Raj said.

"I know," Asha told him, her pace slowing as they reached the pond. The women and children had gone, and the still water gleamed like a mirror in the late-afternoon light.

The cousins walked on in silence until their ancestral home loomed in front of them. "Can you teach me to hit that topspin lob?" Raj asked just before they entered the gate. "It's fabulous. Just like Virginia Wade."

Asha smiled wistfully. "You mean Vijay Amritraj."

She engraved her cousin's words on the back of her mind as she crept upstairs to take a bath. His compliment about her tennis was probably the last nice thing she'd hear from a relative for a long time.

# FIFTEEN

It started during dinner. Uncle, Reet, Raj, and the twins were already sitting, sleeves rolled up, fingers of right hands shaping balls of rice on their plates. Ma, Auntie, Grandmother, and the cook hovered around the table filling plates.

Asha made a late entrance, missing her braid the way a soldier must miss an amputated limb. Her whole family stared at her, openmouthed.

Ma dropped her spoon. "Oh, Bhagavan! Asha! What happened to your hair?" She put her hands along the sides of her own head as though it suddenly weighed too much for her neck.

Asha shrugged and slid into her seat, trying to sound casual. "I cut it off. Girls wear their hair short in America, Ma. I wanted to be ready."

Now Ma lifted both hands in the air. *"Eesh!"* she said. Asha flinched.

"Her hair's all wavy now, Ma," Reet said quickly. "See? Before, it was too heavy for the curls to show. I think it suits her." But she didn't meet Asha's eyes, and Asha sensed her sister's confusion. Usually she would have told Reet before doing anything so rash.

Auntie double-flicked her tongue against her front teeth, making that clicking noise Asha hated almost as much as the word "eesh." "At least her hair used to be beautiful," Auntie said. "Now what does she have?"

Somebody knocked at the front door, and everybody jumped. "Is it the telegram boy?" Grandmother asked urgently.

The housemaid lifted a curtain and peered out of the window. "No," she answered. "Just a neighbor, memsahib."

Raj got up and went into the living room to open the door. "Come in, come in, Uncle," they heard him say. "I'll get my baba for you."

*It could be any older man in the neighborhood,* Asha told herself, her heart pounding. *Raj calls all of them Uncle.*

Uncle hated being interrupted during dinner. After rinsing the curry off his fingers and drying them, he stalked out of the room to greet his guest.

Raj closed the door behind the two men. "It's him," he told Asha in a low voice as he headed back to his seat.

Suddenly the chili pepper Asha had been enjoying seared her tongue. The room was stifling, the air chafed her skin like a wool blanket. The voices in the front room grew louder; then everybody jumped as the front door banged shut. Uncle returned and took his place between Reet and Raj.

Asha didn't look up. Her armpits were starting to itch, and the space between her shoulder blades felt damp.

"Raj, get up," Uncle said grimly. "Sumitra, sit down."

Raj stood up and held out his chair. Ma landed in it with a thump. It wasn't proper for a woman to sit at the dinner table with her older brother-in-law. But Uncle had issued a command, and Ma couldn't disobey him. It was even stranger that he'd called her by name. Now Asha and Ma were sitting beside each other, across the table from Uncle, as though they were on trial. The whole family was silent, even the small cousins.

Uncle started talking. Asha tried to tune out his voice as he recounted the details of her afternoon's activities. But even as the sweat poured down her back, she was impressed by the accuracy of the gossip chain. The length of Raj's stolen shorts was described as *reaching only to the middle of the thigh,* which was exactly right.

"Why did she do this terrible thing?" Uncle demanded. "Haven't we taken your daughters in and treated them as our own?"

Ma's face was blank. She didn't answer.

Uncle turned to Asha. "What do *you* have to say?"

Asha's chair felt like a gas burner with the flame turned up high. She fought the urge to empty the entire pitcher of water over her steaming head. "I—I wanted to stop that fellow from marrying Reet," she said.

"*I* am in charge of this household," Uncle said fiercely. "Don't you think *I* know what's best for your sister?"

*No, I don't,* Asha wanted to respond. But she didn't; it would seal her fate forever. And Ma's, too. "Reet doesn't want to get married," she said instead. "At least, not yet."

"What? She hasn't told me this. Shona, is this true?" Uncle asked.

Reet looked at Ma, whose face was a stone. The Jailor was fully in charge now, and Asha could almost hear a malicious chuckle.

"Well?" Uncle asked again.

Reet reached across the table for her sister's hand. "Uncle, I'm not ready to get married," she said, quietly at first, but her voice gained confidence as she kept on. "Not yet, anyway. When I'm a bit older, I know you and Grandmother and Baba and Ma will find me a wonderful husband."

Uncle frowned. "I was told you were ready. I certainly wouldn't have started this conversation otherwise." His expression softened. "But you *are* growing into a lovely young woman, Shona, and the proposals will begin to come whether you're ready for them or not. We have to start thinking about the best possible match for you before too long." He sat back in his chair and shook his head. "As for your sister, I've never heard of such an unwomanly, disrespectful act in all my life. As though we couldn't handle this situation without her humiliating every boy in town!"

"It's Bintu's fault," Auntie added, dragging Baba's name onto the list of the accused. "He's always treated her like a boy. Teaching her tennis and whatnot. Now my own daughters will have to live in the shadow of this ridiculous behavior. People will think our whole family is mixed up."

Grandmother entered the fray. "Bintu was never the one who taught her how to dress like a boy. Bintu never tried to pretend they had a son. Bintu is not the one to blame for Asha's behavior. Unless you blame him for choosing his wife."

Everybody gasped. Grandmother had never expressed her disapproval of Ma and Baba's unarranged marriage so vehemently. Ma stood up, but Grandmother wasn't finished. "You treated her like a son," she said, blocking Ma's exit. "It's your fault. Look! Just look at how you dressed that poor girl for years." She lifted her hand and made a sweeping wave at the wall behind her.

The framed photos on the dining room wall were so familiar that nobody ever really looked at them closely anymore. But now Asha scrutinized them along with everybody else, wondering what in the world her grandmother was talking about. Slowly, the truth dawned. In most of the photos taken when they were small, Reet was always dressed in frocks and frills, while Asha was wearing shorts. Reet's hair was in braids, but Asha's hair was cropped like a boy's, shorter even than she had just cut it herself. In fact, to a stranger's eyes, those younger versions of her looked much more like a boy than a girl.

Asha had always known that Baba used to treat her like a son. Now, thanks to Grandmother's outburst, it finally dawned on her that it had been Ma who had cut her hair short, Ma who had dressed her in shorts and pants, Ma who had obviously been trying to camouflage in public the fact that she hadn't produced a son for her husband.

The room was quiet; by now everybody had taken in

Grandmother's meaning. Slowly, as though they'd re-hearsed it, every head swiveled to Ma. She endured the scrutiny for only a few moments, and even then the Jailor didn't let her run, or weep, or shout. Gathering her saree around her, she climbed the stairs with a slow, heavy tread.

"Poor thing," Auntie said, but her voice didn't sound sympathetic. "She's never recovered from not giving Bintu a boy."

"It's not surprising," Grandmother added, still angry. "She came from such an uneducated background. I *told* Bintu so many times."

"And now look what's happened to their daughter." Uncle snorted, flicking his head in Asha's direction. "Still pretending to be a boy, after all these years."

"Eesh," said Auntie, wrinkling her nose in disgust.

"*Bas!* That's enough," Grandmother said, ending the discussion.

Asha was a shrieking kettle on the verge of exploding, a fire about to send flames into their faces. She opened her mouth, but Reet's groping foot found hers in the nick of time and pressed down, hard. Asha clamped her lips, re-peating the promises she'd made to Baba in her head like a mantra. *Take care of Ma. Take care of Reet. Don't dishonor Ma.* Pushing her chair away from the table, she excused herself and left the room.

Up, up, and up she climbed, out to the darkness on the roof. A few stars were shining feebly in the smoky sky, the heavy air promising another storm. There was no sign of Jay; his room was dark.

Asha let her hands travel across her slim hips and

waist, curving up her body to the small rise of her breasts. She knew she wasn't half as beautiful as her sister, at least not by Gupta standards, but she had always secretly liked her shape, the way she was blooming slowly, like a lotus flower. Now her flesh felt as stiff and unyielding as wood.

She fingered the bones of her face, her slim neck, the outlines of her skull. *Nothing feminine about my head,* she thought. *No wonder it was easy to fool everybody.* Next, she touched the jagged ends of her hair. It had taken a year and a half to grow that braid. She'd be eighteen, almost nineteen, by the time it was that long again.

The tears came, flowing freely. Asha knew why. It wasn't her hair she was mourning. She was grieving the losses of a small girl, disguised so well that nobody recognized her. Not even herself.

# SIXTEEN

Asha crept downstairs once the house had quieted for the night, slipping under the mosquito net and retucking it under the mattress. Reet and the cousins were already asleep, but Asha found her corner of the hard bed and tossed restlessly.

She was even more furious now about the changes she'd had to endure once her period started. Both of her parents had treated her like a boy, and then in one day expected her to let go of the freedom that came with boyhood. It wasn't fair. They should have readied her for womanhood from the start. Reet had seemed to survive the transition from girlhood just fine; for Asha it had felt like a death sentence.

Asha turned again and again, trying to find a more comfortable place on the mattress, her thoughts racing. The next thing she knew, Reet was stroking her hair to wake her up. "We need to talk," she whispered. "Come into the bathroom for a minute."

"The bathroom?" Asha said, blinking furiously as she crawled out of bed. Her eyes were stinging and puffy; she must have finally fallen asleep just before dawn. "Why do we have to go in there?"

Reet handed her sister a bag of chanachoor. "Privacy. Here, Raj got this for you. If you want to skip breakfast, I can tell them you're not hungry and you're not coming down. You can eat this instead."

"Not in that bathroom, I won't."

It was too smelly in there to eat crunchy peanuts and fried lentils. Grandmother thought it was Auntie's responsibility to supervise the woman who cleaned it. Auntie figured it was Grandmother's. Meanwhile, the stink grew, and the girls usually ducked in and out as fast as they could.

Asha reached under the bed, pulled out her bag, and tucked the chanachoor inside it. She felt a surge of gratitude at Raj's kind gesture.

Reet was waiting at the door. "Hurry, Osh. The twins will be back upstairs any minute to wash up before school."

Asha followed her sister to the bathroom. She leaned over the sink and splashed water on her face to get rid of the salty taste on her lips. The cold water felt good against her hot cheeks and burning eyes. She dried her face and took a deep breath.

And almost passed out.

"Let's get out of here, Reet," she urged, fanning the air in front of her face.

"Tell me why you cut your hair. Whole story." Reet was

trying to hold her breath and talk at the same time, so her words came out sounding choppy.

"I cut it off so I could beat him. So he would hate us. And not want to marry you."

"Oh, Osh," Reet said, ending her breath-holding efforts with a huge sigh. "Thanks. But don't you think I could handle getting him to hate me? Why'd you have to get yourself in trouble? And cut off your gorgeous braid?"

Asha looked into her sister's kind eyes. How could anyone ever hate Reet? And besides, she *hadn't* been sure that her sister could handle the situation. "At least I got to play tennis in India one last time," she said, trying to grin. "And you got the chance to tell Uncle that you're not ready for marriage."

The girls abandoned the bathroom and headed downstairs. Thankfully, the dining room was empty. Only the photos on the wall greeted them. Overlooked for so long, they seemed prominent now.

Reet handed Asha a slice of bread. "Are you angry at her?" she asked.

Asha gripped the knife hard as she spread butter on the bread. "Wouldn't you be? *You* didn't have to live a lie for her sake."

Reet shook her head. "I'm not too sure about that," she murmured.

Her sister's words hardly registered with Asha. The hurt of the night before had hardened into something worse. She never wanted to talk to her mother again. And what about Baba? Why had he just stood by and let Ma dress Asha like a boy—until the Day of First Blood, of course, when all of them had to face the truth? Asha Gupta was a girl, and there was no more hiding the fact from anybody, including themselves.

She swallowed the last bite of the bread and butter and washed it down with tea. "It's a miracle I didn't get ruined. At least I think I didn't."

"You're the opposite of ruined, Osh," Reet said. "In the long run, I think you're better off, actually. You've had a certain kind of freedom to be yourself first, while I . . ."

Her unfinished sentence dangled in the air. She stood up and fingered what was left of Asha's hair. "Anyway, you're creative, sister of mine. Nobody can argue with that. Guess what? You accomplished your mission: I'm not going to have to marry the Y.L.I.! Hooray! When it grows out a bit, I can fix your hair in a new style I saw the other day—pulled to the side with a hairpin. It's perfect for shorter hair."

Asha stayed upstairs for the rest of the day, wishing the room had a door to close and trying to ignore Auntie's "eesh-es" when she walked by the curtain. Ma didn't come up and neither did Grandmother. After a couple of hours of sleep, Asha woke and stretched across the width of the whole bed. It was the first time she'd had the bed to herself in the four months they'd been there, so for once she risked taking out her diary in her room. She needed desperately to confess exactly what she was feeling.

*Maybe Reet's right, in a way. After all, during the first thirteen years of my life, nobody defined me first as a girl—not even myself. That did give me*

*a strange kind of freedom. I remember thinking I*
*could do anything, be anything, go anywhere . . .*
*Perhaps I should be grateful that I was able to*
*become a person before I had to become a woman.*
*Not every girl gets that chance. Still, it makes me*
*sad, but I don't quite know why.*

Someone knocked on the wall beside the curtain. "Come in," Asha called, stashing her diary and pen under her pillow, even though she knew it was Reet. Who else would take the time to knock instead of barging in?

Her sister brought in a tray of luchis and potatoes and cauliflower, along with a couple of slices of fresh lime. "I told them you weren't feeling well," she said. "So don't eat all of it. Ma fixed the tray."

"I'm not really that hungry anyway," Asha said, but she sat up and took the tray on her lap. The luchis smelled delicious, and she squeezed the lime juice over the potatoes and cauliflower as she always did.

Reet watched her eat for a while. "Ma asked about you. She wanted to know if you were feeling better."

"I don't care."

"Don't lie to yourself, Osh, of course you do. And she cares about you. She's just . . ."

"Thinking of herself first, as usual."

Reet shrugged. "Maybe it's better than always trying to make someone else happy." *Like Baba,* Asha thought, popping another bite of potato into her mouth. *And you.*

"I have something to ask you, Osh."

"Anything, Reet," Asha answered.

"Don't answer back to our elders if they keep talking about this, all right?"

"I don't know if I can do that," Asha said. "Auntie especially drives me mad! Is this for your sake, or for Ma's?"

"Both, I suppose. But does it matter?"

Asha sighed. "Not really."

"You'd better come down for tea," Reet said, picking up the tray, which was empty except for the slices of lime. "Your appetite's obviously returned. Besides, if you cower up here, they'll take even longer to stop talking about your escapade."

Her sister was right, Asha thought. The best thing to do might be to pretend that she hadn't done anything wrong, which she hadn't really. She sauntered downstairs once she heard her cousins' shrill voices and the shrieking of the kettle.

Raj stopped her at the foot of the stairs. "My friends are raving about your topspin," he said. "Can you give me a lesson in the garden?"

Asha grinned. "Of course. I owe you a lifetime of tennis. But let's wait a week or two, okay? I'd better not be seen with a racket in my hand until the fuss dies down a bit. And thanks for the chanachoor, by the way."

After Raj's request, Asha was able to walk into the living room with her head high. Ma was nowhere in sight, and Asha managed to sip her tea quietly while Auntie, Grandmother, and Uncle debated the possible social consequences of her actions. Asha tried to tune them out by remembering the thwack of the ball against the racket as she hit that last lob. Maybe what she'd told Reet was true; she'd endure a lot just to have experienced the sheer joy of playing tennis again. *And* winning.

Over the next couple of weeks, Asha somehow endured her disgrace without a word. Family cardplaying was put on hold, and she found herself missing the strategy discussions and teasing that accompanied it. Grandmother's stern demeanor, Uncle's disapproving glares, Auntie's many "eesh-es" aimed in Asha's direction were all irritating, as was having to forsake playing with her cousins. But they didn't compare to her mother's glum, expressionless face, the sight of which made Asha's nerves twang like a frayed sitar string. This time, though, Asha didn't try any of her tactics to battle the Jailor. She was tired of fighting him, at least for a while, promise or no promise.

One afternoon, the relatives abruptly stopped discussing Asha's "unwomanly" behavior. The college had posted midyear exam scores, and Raj was forced to disclose his failing marks in math. This new calamity proved to be a grand diversion. Now Auntie avoided interactions with the family, throwing angry looks in her son's direction. Grandmother stopped glaring at Ma and clicked her tongue at Auntie instead.

Soon after that, at breakfast, Uncle patted Asha's hand

in an affectionate way that almost reminded Asha of Baba. "How's the best tennis player in the neighborhood?" he asked. "I hear you upheld the family honor on the court quite nicely."

Asha almost fainted.

"You should have seen her, Baba!" Raj burst out. "Those passing shots! That spin she puts on her second serve!"

"I'd like to learn the game myself," Uncle said, stroking his rounded belly. "Maybe I'd lose a couple of kilos."

Asha looked at Ma, who was pouring more tea into Raj's cup. If Uncle's brain had gone through some strange transformation, would the same effect take place in hers? But Ma's face stayed vacant.

"Let's have a game of twenty-nine tonight, eh, Tuni?" Uncle asked. "It's been a while. I've missed it."

After Ma and Uncle left the room, Asha turned to Raj. "What happened to your father?" she asked. "How did I make it back into the family again?"

"Now Baba's sorry he even met with the Y.L.I.'s uncle," Raj informed her. "Yesterday he found out that they have a distant connection to the Mitra clan. Our family's despised them for generations."

"Wonderful," Asha said sarcastically, slumping back into her chair. "So I didn't need my stupid plan after all. I could have waited until an Ancient Hatred returned to rescue my sister."

"That guy needed to be put in his place," Raj said. "And now the whole family has accepted how Reet feels about getting married. Baba might have started looking for another eligible fellow if you hadn't given your sister the chance to say what she thought."

Asha took another big bite of toast, feeling a new lightness of spirit. Raj was right. What else could she have hoped for? Reet *had* managed to speak for herself. And Asha had been given—or had taken—the chance to play tennis again. It had been worth it.

Now only two things were still worrying her. No, three. One was Baba, taking forever to find a job. The second was Ma, thoroughly at the mercy of the Jailor. And the third was Jay. He had disappeared; there had been no sign of him for days. Where was he? Why hadn't he told her he was going to be away? The worst part about these three worries was that she had no Plan A or Plan B to deal with any of them. All she could muster was the energy and courage to wait, which was the hardest plan of all.

# SEVENTEEN

With Reet's proposal gone and the gloomy, quiet Ma back, Auntie wasn't having as much fun. She entered the fray against the Jailor, urging Ma to try on sarees, sing, or go out shopping again. Halfheartedly, Ma finally agreed to a shopping trip, and Auntie commandeered Raj once again to hail the rickshaw and carry the bags.

Reet and Asha stayed home this time, sitting with their grandmother on the veranda and slapping at mosquitoes that nibbled their ankles. The house was quiet and dim; Uncle had taken the twins to the market, and the servants hadn't turned on any lights before leaving for the day. This was at Grandmother's insistence; the family always waited until true darkness came to use the expensive electric lights. Besides, mosquitoes swarmed the open gutters at dusk, and lights drew them into the house.

It was peaceful knowing that only three members of the family were at home, with no servants around. The shadowy figure in the corner that was Grandmother broke the silence. "I wish you girls could have known your grandfather," she said. "He was a fine man, a good father and husband. My parents picked well. I'll never forget our wedding night."

Reet was about to speak, Asha could tell. She tapped her sister's hand once in warning and Reet sat back, both girls waiting for their grandmother to continue.

"I was so scared that day," Grandmother said. "I'd heard such horror stories from my cousins and friends about what happened on a girl's wedding night. I was only fifteen, and your grandfather was twenty-six. He was already a professor, so handsome, tall, and strong."

Again, Asha kept silent, and this time Reet followed suit without a hand tap.

"I haven't slept well in weeks," Grandmother said, and Asha worried for a moment, but their grandmother's mind returned to the olden days. "Before my wedding day, I couldn't sleep, either, I was so scared. The morning was a blur, the putting on of jewelry, the painting of my face with turmeric powder. And then, in the afternoon, after tea, the shouts came from outside: *The bridegroom's coming! He's here! The bridegroom and his procession are here!* I thought I was going to faint." She made a small, tinkly sound, and Asha realized it was the first time she'd heard her grandmother laugh since they'd arrived.

"Later I had to leave my parents' home. Oh, how I wept! I rode with his mother in a rickshaw, and she was talking the entire time. I didn't hear a word she said. The house was full of strangers, laughing, staring, making comments about how I looked, touching my skin, saree, hair. They paraded us into the room that would be our living quarters, and I saw that the wedding bed had been decorated with sweet-smelling jasmine flowers. They left us alone, but I could hear them joking outside, eavesdropping on us."

Asha couldn't see her grandmother at all; it was now completely dark in the room. She pictured a petite teenager perched on the edge of an unfamiliar bed next to a strange man. She felt the girl's terror shiver through her own body.

"Then he started talking," Grandmother said, and her voice broke. "He told me that he'd waited so long for his bride. He'd wait longer, for weeks, or months even, until I was ready to accept him as my husband. He promised not to touch me until I wanted him as much as he wanted me. When we fell asleep that night, I remember feeling completely safe. And he kept his word."

*How long did he have to wait?* Asha wanted to ask, thinking of Jay and feeling her cheeks get hot. *How did it feel when you finally did want him as much as he wanted you?*

But the telling of secrets was over. The girls could hear their grandmother blowing her nose, and the rustle of her saree as she stood up. "Turn on the lights, girls, will you? I'm feeling sleepy for the first time in days. I think I'll go and try to rest."

"Amazing," Reet said as they followed their grandmother inside and Asha switched on the lamp in the living room. "She really misses him."

"I miss him, as well," Asha said. She wondered how his kind, literary presence would affect the household were he still around. She couldn't imagine it.

The girls were switching on the last electric light when Raj and the two daughters-in-law of the house returned, laden with purchases. Raj looked exhausted, hair askew, semicircles of sweat staining his shirt under each arm. He rolled his eyes at Asha and escaped upstairs, muttering something about taking a bath.

Asha studied the jumble of shopping bags on the floor. "Auntie must have encouraged her to buy everything she set her eyes on," she said in a low voice to Reet. "Well, at least Ma's talking again. I wish it were always that easy."

Grandmother stormed into the living room and re-gained control of her galaxy. "Why are you spending so much money, Sumitra?" she demanded. "We must save every penny these days, you know that. We can't afford ex-cesses like this!" Grandmother's lectures always rose to a crescendo before descending into a prayer. "Bintu must get his family settled soon! How I wish his father were still alive! Oh, Bhagavan!"

After invoking God's name in tears, she left the room, heading for her shrine to place more offerings there for her son's sake. Before, Asha had always wondered if the other statues of divinities felt neglected because the goddess of wealth got most of Grandmother's goodies. This time, though, after carrying the ache of her grandfather's ab-sence, she felt sadness for her grandmother instead of scorn.

There was an empty silence, but soon Auntie, who had

experienced firsthand the Wrath of the Mother-in-Law, tried to bring back Ma's short-lived animation. She poured her sister-in-law a cup of tea and begged Reet to sing for them. "You sing and dance almost as well as your mother," she said cleverly.

But Ma's fingers were tying and untying the end of her saree into a knot and her face was void again. Reet started to sing, her eyes on Ma, while Auntie accompanied her on the harmonium. *Knot. Unknot.* Ma's fingers weren't keeping the rhythm; her feet weren't tapping the beat as they did when she wasn't being held captive.

Reet's song was making Auntie sniff over her harmonium. When the music and Reet's high, sweet voice ended on the same note and the song was over, Auntie wiped away tears with her saree.

Asha heard the rumble of Uncle's voice as he deposited groceries in the kitchen and the quick slaps of the cousins' bare feet on the stairs as they headed to their room.

Grumbling at the lateness of the hour, Grandmother quickly fried some okra and reheated lentils and rice. Ma went through the motions of serving the family with Auntie, but her face stayed blank; Reet's song hadn't made a bit of difference.

Grandmother, Uncle, Raj, and the little girls ate quickly and left the table. Reet and Asha were almost done when Ma and Auntie sat down to join them. Auntie glanced at her sister-in-law's drooping figure and gave it one last try. "That woman who cleans the toilets is terrible," she said. "Should we fire her?"

"No, no," Reet said quickly. "You should give her a raise. She'll work harder then."

"Sumitra," Auntie said. "What do *you* think we should do? Your husband always told us how you managed your home so well in Delhi."

To Asha's amazement, this odd intervention, too, was temporarily successful. Ma straightened up and pulled her plate closer. "Fire her, of course," she said. "The toilet in this house smells horrible. My girl in Delhi always kept the bathroom spotless. More money won't make a bit of difference."

*Brought back by a smelly toilet,* Asha thought. *At least until the next blow.* She was grateful that Auntie had joined their side for a while in the never-ending battle. She herself still needed a break.

"Tuni Didi! Come upstairs *now*! We're wa-a-a-iting for you!"

The chorus of voices was persistent, and Asha responded, racing upstairs with a loud roar for the usual bedtime romp.

# EIGHTEEN

Late-afternoon sunlight was flooding the roof, warming Asha's skin. She drank in the solitude and calm and stretched her legs out, pretending she was one of the lizards basking in the last sunshine. Inside, these tik-tiki darted into dark corners at the first sign of a human being. Up here, though, they didn't seem to mind her company.

It was September, and Calcutta was on the brink of cooler harvest days and festivals; the monsoon would be leaving before she did. It was perfect cricket weather; maybe Raj wanted to practice in the garden until it got dark. Where was he, anyway? Probably lying low to avoid another lecture about his poor study habits. Or maybe he was keeping an eye out for that girl who paraded past the house every day, hips swishing under her salwar kameez as though she knew Raj was watching.

The cousins could use a practice session of cards, too, even though they were getting better at twenty-nine. The other night, Asha and Raj had actually won a round against his parents for the first time. The whole family, including Uncle and Auntie, had cheered loudly—except Ma, who stayed cloistered in her tiny room. Afterward, as Sita and Suma pummeled Asha with pillows and then ran squealing through the house, Asha had felt a strange sensation of timelessness, as though she'd been living in this ancestral home forever. Their time in Delhi, with Kavita, Bishop Academy, and Baba, which had ended months earlier, felt like a dream.

Asha turned to scrutinize Jay's house. He'd been missing for three weeks, the shutters of his window closed tightly, and she hadn't glimpsed him inside or outside the house. She hadn't gathered the courage to ask anybody about him, either, although she'd been tempted to offer the sweeper who worked for both of their houses a rupee in exchange for information.

As though the intensity of her desire had summoned him, the window across the way flew open. Jay's face, haggard and sporting a beard, grinned at her as though he'd just seen her the day before. "Osh!" he called triumphantly. "I'm done!"

"Shhh. Someone will hear you. Where have you been?"

"Here. Inside. Painting. And I'm finished."

"You've been painting all this time? I thought you'd gone somewhere."

"I've been living down in the servants' quarters finishing up the portrait. I didn't want to be distracted, Osh. I knew if you were out here, I'd want to talk to you instead of paint, so I made myself move to the other side of the house."

"You could have told me."

"I'm sorry, I should have, but I was in the thick of it then. Possessed by the painting. I wasn't thinking of anything else."

"Not even me?" She spoke the words without thinking about how brash they might sound.

He smiled. "Not even you. I've sent it off posthaste to a gallery in Delhi."

"*What?* I didn't even get a peek, Jay."

"How could you, Osh? You'd have had to come over here, and you know that's impossible."

"You could have held it up to the window."

"I didn't want to risk my parents seeing it if I carried it back upstairs. They'd know I'd been painting you, and they wouldn't be pleased. So I wrapped it in paper and hauled it to the post office. I just got back. The gallery's been wanting me to send them a portrait for months. They're going to show it to international art dealers from around the world. Wouldn't it be wonderful if someone wanted to display it in one of the galleries I used to visit in Paris when I was studying there?"

"But it's of me. *Me.* I should have seen it, Jay."

Jay was flying so high with euphoria that he didn't notice how upset Asha was.

"You will, Osh. I'll take you to Paris when it's hanging in the Louvre, and we'll see it together."

Her heart thump-thumped. That was more like it; her anger ebbed. "We will?"

"Definitely."

"It's *come!*" A shriek rocked the house, and Asha jumped. What was going on? Why was Grandmother shouting like that?

"Telegram! Sumitra! Bontu! Where are you?"

"It's Baba! He must have found a job!" Asha flashed Jay a smile and barreled down the stairs two at a time, stumbling once, catching herself on the banister.

This was it. Finally. Baba had come through; he was sending for them; they would escape the prison of this house forever. And someday Jay's fame would bring him to New York, where he would seek her out, she was sure of it. She felt like singing and dancing with joy.

Reet raced breathlessly into the living room and took Asha's hand. Grandmother was holding a slip of paper in her hand and a ripped envelope in the other. Ma and Auntie joined them, followed by Raj, Uncle, and the cousins.

"I can't make sense of it," Grandmother said, handing it to Uncle. "It's in English."

"Read it quickly, brother," Ma said, breaking a youngest-wife-in-the-household rule for the first time and actually ordering her brother-in-law to do something.

Nobody reacted to her breach of conduct; every eye was riveted on the telegram. Uncle read it silently. Asha watched his face grow as blank as an erased chalkboard. He crumpled the telegram in his fist and still didn't say word. Suddenly Asha knew; her heart was inside his hand along with that foreign piece of paper.

"What's wrong?" Grandmother asked, her voice trembling. "Tell us now, Bontu."

"It's not from him at all," Uncle said. "It's from the police department in New York City. He's—he's—" He stopped, and his eyes darted from his mother, to his sister-in-law, to his nieces before he managed to say the two words they were by now all dreading: "He's dead."

For the rest of her life, Asha would replay what happened in that room where her father had crawled as a baby, laughed with his brother in his youth, and embraced his mother countless times.

Grandmother swayed before falling, and Uncle ran to catch her. Reet went to Ma and guided her to the sofa, where they sat down. The little cousins began to cry; Auntie gathered them close. Raj stood apart, his head bowed. Somewhere in the distance a wounded mongoose began to shriek, stung by the cobra it was trying to kill. It took Asha a minute to realize that the high-pitched wail was coming out of her own mouth, and then everything went dark.

# NINETEEN

ASHA WAS UNDER HER MOSQUITO NET, AND REET'S BODY WAS curled tightly against her back. Each deep, steady breath her sister exhaled stirred the hair on the back of Asha's skull. Moonlight flooded the room, and rising up on one elbow, she could make out the dim forms of Sita's and Suma's bodies on the other side of the bed. Everything seemed normal, but suddenly she realized that she was still wearing the salwar kameez she'd put on the morning before.

So the telegram hadn't been the worst nightmare of her life.

It was real.

Baba was gone.

He had died in a train station, jostled by the crowd off the platform and onto the electric rail, dead in seconds after the shock had ravaged his nervous system. That was what Asha thought she remembered, but vaguely, as Uncle had made phone call after phone call trying to gather information. Maybe her sister knew more.

"Reet, Reet, Reet," Asha said, shaking her sister and trying not to wake the twins. It didn't work; Reet didn't stir.

Asha lifted the mosquito net and scanned the small table beside the bed. She dimly remembered coming into consciousness, taking three pills, and drinking the glass of water Uncle handed her. Sure enough, a bottle of pills and an empty glass stood there. How many of those had they made her sister swallow? Reet was still in oblivion; the three they'd given Asha hadn't lasted through the night. How many did you need before you never woke up again, never saw your rumpled salwar kameez, never realized that your father had fallen on an electric rail and was no longer there?

Had he felt pain? Had the volts of electricity fried his body, brain, bones, blood? Fighting the urge to scream, Asha counted out three pills and swallowed them quickly. Then she tucked herself back into the curve of her sister's body, put a pillow over her head, and waited for sleep to take her again.

The Jailor easily seized all three of them. A heavy numbness displaced Asha's despair the next time she woke. It was so bulky that it didn't allow her to cry, scream, utter even two words. Both her sister and her mother were equally lifeless, the three of them managing the motions of eating, sitting, sleeping, and bathing in a silent daze.

*I'm suffocating,* Asha thought at least thirty times a day, longing to run up to the roof so that she could breathe. But she didn't. She stayed by her sister's side, and they flanked their silent mother like statues.

They could hear Grandmother sobbing in her prayer room, and a pill bottle like the one the girls reached for at night was on their grandmother's dresser. Only their mother refused Uncle's gift of medicated oblivion, and soon dark half circles discolored the flesh under her eyes.

Servants hauled piles of colorful silk and cotton out of Ma's room, and Ma had to borrow one of Grandmother's white sarees until she could buy one or two of her own. She could never again wear anything but white, the color of mourning that implied that a widow, too, was dead. Dully, Asha registered Auntie tucking away the most expensive of Ma's sarees in a trunk. The day after the telegram came, Ma stopped adorning the part in her hair with the stripe of vermilion powder. The unfamiliar exposed quarter-inch line of skin across her mother's scalp reminded Asha of a scar. Weeping, Grandmother and Auntie led Ma to the pond so she could break her marriage bangles in half and throw them into the water. With her bare wrists and scalp bereft of color, it seemed to Asha that their mother, too, was becoming a ghost.

"The body?" Ma asked Uncle once. Those were the only two words the girls heard her speak during the required thirteen days before the memorial.

"His friends will have it burned in New York. One of

them is coming in a month or so, and he'll bring the ashes for you and the girls to give to Mother Ganga. Beta, take this."

Raj stared in confusion at the razor his father was holding. "But, Baba, I already have one."

Uncle sighed. "You'll have to shave your head. For your uncle's memorial."

Asha stood up immediately. "I'll do it," she said, taking the razor from her cousin's hand. "He's my baba."

"You can't shave your head, Tuni," Uncle said, and his voice was so gentle that for the first time it sounded exactly like Baba's. "Only a son can make that sacrifice. Without a son, a nephew must take the duty."

Asha nodded, too drained of strength to protest. Besides, a simple shaving of the head didn't come close to demonstrating the overwhelming grief she was carrying inside.

# TWENTY

JAY CAME TO THE MEMORIAL SERVICE WITH HIS PARENTS, clean-shaven and dressed in a formal kurta and pajama, like all the other men who attended. Asha didn't look his way, but as he passed her in the dark hallway he glanced quickly around, reached for her hand, and squeezed it, hard. It was the first time they'd touched, and he let go quickly as the hall filled up with other visitors. Tears filled Asha's eyes for the first time since the telegram, but she blinked them back quickly. Reet was the only one who noticed Jay's gesture, and apart from a quick intake of breath, she didn't say anything.

The rest of the day was a blur to Asha. She stayed close to her sister and blocked out Grandmother's wailing and crying, the scores of proverbs and platitudes offered by neighbors and relatives, and the priest's intoned prayers for Baba's incarnation into the next life. Reet and Ma were managing the correct social motions, too, greeting visitors, nodding, pretending to listen, but Asha could tell they were in the grip of the same terrible numbness. *So this is the power that captures Ma,* she thought. *No wonder it takes so much to free her.*

That night, she stopped taking the medication. Once her sister was asleep, palm to palm with both hands between cheek and pillow as usual, Asha forced herself to picture Baba's face. The image that came first was one of his cheeks crinkling in laughter after he told a funny story; the girls always teased him about laughing more than his listeners at his own jokes. The salty tears came silently at first; then Asha released deep, rending sobs into her pillow while Reet slept on. After hours of crying, sleep finally came, but it wasn't deep, and Asha woke again to fresh tears.

Every moment she could, she scribbled memories of Baba in her diary. Jokes he'd told, advice he'd given, times just the two of them had sipped tea and talked about tennis. Asha made herself remember, chiseling away at the numbness bit by bit. It was the most difficult thing she'd ever done, allowing herself to suffer a pain she could barely tolerate. The days were easier because her diary absorbed some of it. Nights were rough; four times she failed, groping in the dark for the nightstand, finding and taking the pills.

But the Jailor was reluctantly loosening his grip on her, and she kept at it. The only thing she chased from her mind was imagining Baba's last minutes of life. What good would it do to try to travel where her own memory couldn't take her?

Baba's last postcard arrived the day after the memorial. Asha saw it on the veranda where the postman had left the mail, grabbed it, and raced with it up to the roof. She wanted to read it alone, so for once she was glad there was no sign of Jay.

The picture was of the Verrazano-Narrows Bridge, and Baba's message was brief:

*Dear Shona and Tuni,*

*I can't wait to see your sweet faces again; I miss you and love you more than life itself. Remember the promises you made, my beloved daughters. Take care of each other and your ma. Soon I'll send for you, very soon.*

*As ever, I remain*
*your loving Baba*

Asha read it three times, pain searing through her like a sword. She put her head down on her knees and wept in the daylight, trying her best to be quiet so nobody would hear.

The windows across the way opened slowly. "Osh, do you need me?" Jay asked, his voice gentle.

She wiped her nose and eyes on her scarf and looked up. Slowly, she nodded. "You've got to help me, Jay. I have to take care of Ma and Reet. I promised my baba."

"I'll do anything, Osh. Anything. Just tell me and I'll do it."

"For now, stay here for a while with me, will you?"

He did, sitting by the open window and letting her cry, and cry, and cry.

Finally she stood up. "I have to show Reet this postcard, but I think it might kill her. It's the last one he wrote."

"Jay! Time for tea!" It was his mother's voice from below, and he gave Asha one last encouraging smile before they each went to their respective downstairs.

Reet took Baba's card and read it silently, but even then she didn't cry. "Can I keep this one?" she asked Asha. "You've got seven; I've only got six."

Asha nodded. The day before they had divided up Baba's postcards like jewels; it was the most extensive discussion the sisters had had since the news had come. Reet was using fewer and fewer words as the days went by. She'd nod, shrug, or shake her head; it was as though the Jailor were squeezing her tongue between two iron fingers.

The days plodded on into October, and then November, but the family wouldn't participate in any festivals this year. No birthdays, holy days, or other celebrations. In mourning, the family also had to relinquish meat and fish for a month, and the cook grumbled over the extra cleaning of the utensils to ensure a vegetarian kitchen. Ma, according to custom, was supposed to give up meat and fish forever.

Asha made herself chew and swallow lentils, eggplant, rice, potatoes, noticing that her sister was eating next to nothing. Ma was eating, but automatically, as though somebody else were in charge of what her hand was bringing to her mouth. No sign of tears from either of them, but by now Asha was crying enough for forty daughters, mothers, and wives. She shared the job with Grandmother, who wept ferociously in front of her gods and goddesses day and night.

The balance of power in the house was shifting so fast that Asha sometimes wondered if the old building itself was actually tilting. Grandmother was fading, dwindling, disappearing for hours with her inconsolable sorrow into the prayer room. Auntie, meanwhile, soon stopped pretending to grieve. Asha didn't mind that; after all, Raj's mother had hardly known Baba. What the girls did mind was the way she began treating Ma. Gone were the days of giggling and gossiping as if they were friends, or trying delicately to cajole Ma back into a better mood. Now it was: "Stop sulking, Sumitra. You're a bad example to my girls." Or: "Can't you remind your daughters to make the bed upstairs after they get up? The servants are complaining about how lazy they are."

Ma never answered Auntie back or argued. In fact, she hardly spoke at all. The few times she talked to the girls or answered one of Grandmother's direct questions, she didn't use the high Bangla of the upper-class Delhi circles that she'd perfected. Now only the village version of the language came out of her mouth, as though she'd lost the desire to pretend along with her status as Baba's wife.

Asha kept going only because of the promises she'd made to Baba. But how could she keep them? She felt more powerless and lonely than the girl Jay had sketched on the roof. The strange sight of Ma without makeup, bangles, or any color adorning her face and body was enough to make the tears come again. Not to mention her sister, sitting silently in a dark corner with all seven of her postcards spread across her lap. Reet's curves were slipping away like the tides of the sea, the bones in her neck and shoulders jutting out like rocks.

Asha tried taking her diary up to the roof but stopped writing once Jay appeared. Then she'd start to talk while he listened, telling him story after story about her father. After a while, they even laughed over some of the funny things Baba had said and done, both of them with tears in their eyes. She could see Jay's eyes because he leaned so far out of his window, almost as though he were trying to reach her. But the houses, close enough for conversation, were too far for touching.

# TWENTY-ONE

WHEN BABA'S ASHES WERE BROUGHT TO INDIA A MONTH AF-
ter his death, it was the girls' duty to take them to the
Ganges River. Uncle and Raj went with them, but as was the
custom, Ma, Grandmother, Auntie, and the little girls
stayed at home. Their uncle and cousin led the way in one
rickshaw and the sisters rode in another, the carton from
America cradled in Reet's lap. A priest met them on the cement stairs that descended into the river, built for just this
purpose, and a crowd of strangers gathered to watch.

Uncle stood on the top step, water sloshing around his
shoes, and opened the box. He handed Reet the large urn
that was inside, and then he and Raj waited while the girls
climbed down four more steps. Reet's saree floated around
her knees; Asha's salwar became so heavy it felt as if the

current were trying to drag her downstream. Maybe she would let it if it tugged fiercely enough.

The sisters didn't look at each other before reaching in to pick up handfuls of what was left of their father. As they scattered his ashes over the river, Asha heard her sister finally beginning to cry, a high-pitched sound of sorrow rising above the horns of the passing barges. Asha wept, too, and her tears this time weren't for Baba, but for the two of them, desolate as the water flowed around them, taking Baba's body away from them forever.

When they got back, neighbors were gathered on the corner outside the house, obviously in the middle of a gossip session. Ma was waiting just inside the gate, which was unusual, as she'd rarely ventured outside the house since their arrival in Calcutta and had never left it once the telegram had arrived.

The neighbors stopped in midsentence as the Gupta girls disembarked from the rickshaw.

"Wonder what they're talking about," Asha said dully as their mother opened the gate to let them in. "Did I wear the wrong colors or something?"

"No," Ma answered, taking the empty urn from Reet. "You girls are dressed appropriately. I've been through this before, remember?"

It was an obscure reference to the Strangers. Asha pictured a younger version of Ma strewing her own father's ashes, and then her mother's, over a faraway bend of the river as it curved down from the Himalayan foothills.

"I know what they're saying," Reet said as the gate closed behind them. "It's about Baba."

Ma stopped. "What about him?" she asked. "What have you heard, Shona?"

"They're saying that it wasn't an accident, Ma."

"What?" Asha asked.

"The gossip—the gossip is that Baba couldn't find a job. That he lost hope. That—that he jumped on that track because he gave up." Reet's voice broke and she began to cry again. Ma handed the urn to Asha and put her arms around her older daughter.

Clutching the empty container tightly, Asha kicked the gate as hard as she could. She didn't care that the neighbors were gaping at her. "It's not true!" she said. "He wrote that last card just before it happened and said he was sending for us soon. Besides, Baba would never do something that terrible to us."

"Your sister's right, Shona," Ma said, steering Reet slowly toward the house. "They don't know your father; we do. He would never have left us like this. Never."

Conviction rang in her voice, and Reet's sobs slowed. "I knew they were wrong, but when the cook told me what she'd overheard, I couldn't help being afraid. I'm sorry, Ma. Osh. You're right. We *know* Baba."

Head high, Asha strode down the path behind her sister and mother as the neighbors watched them go.

Inside the house, Ma fell silent again, but Asha clung to the memory of her brief reappearance at the gate when they'd needed her most.

The age-old ritual at the Ganges had helped Reet to start grieving, and her tears flowed freely now. Asha was beyond grateful, because seeing Reet in a stupor had terrified her; she'd felt as though her sister, too, had left her.

Weeping reminded them that they, at least, were still alive, and the sisters began to do a lot of it. They locked themselves in the bathroom, or stayed hidden under the mosquito net, talking, reminiscing, and crying until they fell asleep, curled up so closely it felt as if Reet's heart were beating inside Asha's body.

"Why don't you eat, Reet?" Asha asked one night. She tapped on each rib through the skin on her sister's back.

"I can't. I try, but I feel like vomiting with every bite. I'll have to get some new clothes. Nothing fits anymore."

"Your bra hangs on you like a boy's kurta."

"And I've stopped bleeding."

"What?"

"My period hasn't come in two months, Osh."

"So that's why I haven't seen any rags but mine and Ma's hanging on the line. The twins haven't started yet; lucky them, and I think Auntie's done."

"That's been the only good part—not having to wash out those disgusting rags."

"Tell Ma; maybe you need to see a doctor."

"What good will that do? It will just worry her even more, and she doesn't have money for a doctor—she used the last bit Baba left her for those sarees. And I hate to ask Uncle."

"I know. We're totally dependent on him now. Oh, how I hate it."

"Maybe Baba left some money behind for us, but how do we find out?"

"I have no idea," Asha said. "We can't ask Ma. The Jailor loves it when someone brings up money in front of her."

But Uncle brought up the subject himself one afternoon over tea, clearing his throat and taking a deep breath as though he needed extra courage for what he was about to say. "Bintu didn't leave much behind," he told Ma. "The last bit in his bank account paid for the memorial."

"So we have nothing left?" Ma asked, eyes wide.

"You have the girls' dowries," Uncle said gruffly. "We would never touch those. And you have us. This house is your house as long as I'm alive. And then my son will provide for you."

Raj chimed in: "I will, I promise. And the girls, too."

Auntie was frowning down at her cup of tea but didn't say anything.

Grandmother shook her head. "How we'll manage, I don't know," she said, wiping her eyes on a corner of her saree again. "We've barely kept this house running after Bintu stopped sending money from Delhi; our own savings have gotten quite low."

Auntie's head flew up. "My husband makes enough to support his family," she said sharply.

Nobody spoke.

"We'll have to get rid of a couple of the servants," Uncle said finally. "We can't do without the sweeper or the washerwoman, so Babu and the cook will have to go."

"And who will do *their* work?" Auntie asked.

"We all will," Grandmother answered.

"I can cook," Ma said quickly.

"And Asha and I can take over most of Babu's work," Reet added. "We can make the beds and burn the garbage."

"No!" Grandmother said sharply. "I won't have any member of our family doing such a low job as garbage burning. We can afford to hire a boy who lives by the river to do it. And Sumitra, we'll all cook together. I won't have the neighbors accusing me of exploiting you."

"I've never cooked in my life," Auntie said. "*My* father employed a dozen servants and two cooks."

"Well, you'll learn now," Uncle said dryly. "It's never too late."

Raj made a restless sound. "I'd better go study," he said, and left the room.

Asha guessed he was weighing the new load of providing for six women instead of three.

# TWENTY-TWO

It helped to work around the house, so work they did. Reet made the beds so perfectly you could bounce a spoon on them; Sita and Suma tried it and actually caught a spoon in the air. And once the cook had left, Ma spent long hours in the kitchen, grinding spices, chopping onions, kneading luchi dough, and stirring up curries that were more savory than anything the cook had ever produced.

"This eggplant dish is delicious," Uncle said over dinner, ignoring his wife's sour expression.

"I suppose you cooked in your village," Auntie said.

"Every day," Ma answered. "My mother taught me how."

"Oh."

The word was innocent but the two-syllable tone dripped with meaning, and Asha was peeved on behalf of one of the Strangers.

Ma's face didn't change. She answered when spoken to, was polite, and still made sure her daughters were properly dressed and groomed. But there was no anger in her expression, or sadness, or laughter. Her face was like a mask that robbers put on to disguise their true identities. She never argued, or scolded the girls, or offered an opinion. The only signs of grief were the dark half-moons under her eyes and the deepening lines on her forehead, which had never been there before. She was wearing one of Grandmother's old white sarees; Asha knew their mother would never ask Uncle to buy her a new one, and he didn't offer. But the saree wouldn't last forever, unlike Ma's time to mourn.

Asha couldn't figure out how she could help earn her keep around the house. "I've got to find a way to make myself valuable," she told Jay one afternoon.

"You're extremely valuable," he said.

"No, I mean under this roof," she said, stomping her foot on the cement for emphasis. "If all I'm doing is consuming and not contributing anything, I'll have no power at all. At least Ma's cooking for them now, even though Auntie's ordering her around just like she used to boss Babu and the cook. Uncle absolutely loves Ma's cooking, which drives Auntie crazy but gives Ma something, at least."

"And your sister?"

"She makes the beds, entertains the twins, and sings when they ask her to. Plus she's good at managing the sweeper and washerwoman. The servants are starting to come to her with questions now instead of Auntie; they're scared to death of Grandmother."

"You read to the cousins and tell stories," Jay said. "I can hear your voice when we're at tea. I can't quite make out the words, but because the girls don't interrupt I'm sure they're listening."

"They do like that, but I want to do something for this family that makes me *indispensable.* I can't stand feeling like I'm the recipient of charity—like one of those beggars at the marketplace."

Jay shook his head. "I tried to paint a beggar once, but it was too painful when I got to the eyes. I had to stop."

"Then you see why I want to find something to do around here that they value."

"I'll try to think of something, Osh."

For days, Asha wandered aimlessly, straightening the shoes on the veranda, dusting windowsills that were already clean, getting underfoot in the kitchen with her efforts to help until Ma and Grandmother scolded her out. She was useless at housework, she realized. But what could she do instead?

Her chance came when her cousin was studying in his room late one night. She heard him groan through the closed door as she walked by, and she hesitated, then knocked. "Raj? What's wrong?"

"It's this disgusting proof. I can't understand one word of it."

She walked in. "Let me see."

He brought another chair into his room, and Asha sat down beside him at his desk. She explained the proof step by step until Raj's eyes lit up. "I see it!" he crowed. "You're good, Osh. Our professor never made it this clear. I actually understand it."

"I can go over geometry with you anytime, Raj," she said eagerly. "When's your next exam?"

"Two weeks. If you help me, Osh, maybe I won't fail this time."

"Fail? You're going to get top marks, cousin of mine."

When the results came in, her prediction was proved right. Raj's parents beamed as they perused the exam list, spotting their son's name fifth from the top instead of smack at the bottom. "How can this be?" his mother asked in wonder.

"It was Osh," Raj said immediately. "She studied with me. She's a great teacher, Ma."

Auntie's eyes narrowed as she surveyed her niece, who was reading to Sita and Suma. "Really? Well, maybe she'd like to tutor my girls, too. What do you say, Tuni?"

"I'd love to, Auntie," Asha answered. It was the first time in weeks that her aunt had asked her for something instead of commanding it.

Later, she overheard her grandmother talking in a low voice. "You would have had to pay for a tutor for that boy."

"And for the girls, too," Auntie answered. "That daughter of Bintu's is a smart one."

Asha smiled. It was a first step in her Baba-promise-keeping strategy—not a huge one, maybe, but it felt better than losing ground.

The twins, of course, were thrilled. They craved time with either of their cousins like extra sugar in their daily glass of milk. Now every afternoon they sat with Asha while she reviewed their schoolwork with them. And she made it fun, inventing games and coming up with small prizes to spur them on—ten more minutes to play hide-and-seek before bedtime, two of Reet's uneaten biscuits from tea, an extra Grimms' story, the chance to try any hairstyle they wanted on Reet's head.

Sita was a bit better at math, while Suma seemed to have more skill with language, but both girls learned slowly, Asha realized. It took creativity and patience to help them grasp a concept, and when she couldn't fall asleep at night, she found herself coming up with new ways to teach.

What with tutoring the twins and helping Raj study, she didn't have as much time to go up to the roof. She'd seen Jay only briefly, bringing him up to date on her efforts to restore the balance of power under their roof.

One afternoon he had some news of his own. "I got a letter today, Osh," he told her. "From a university in America. In New York, to be exact."

Asha winced at the mention of the city she had almost called home. Her father's death place. "What did it say?"

"Apparently one of the professors there saw my paintings in Delhi, and he's offered me a full scholarship to study in their fine arts program. I could become a teacher and keep painting. They've offered me a studio, housing, transportation, everything."

Her stomach turned over. Would he be leaving? "That's wonderful, Jay!" Somehow, she managed to sound delighted. "When will you go?"

"I'm not going," he said. "I haven't even told my parents about it."

"Why in the world not?"

"I'm an Indian, Osh. If I move to America, I'll lose . . . all this." He gestured across the coconut trees, the pond gleaming in the afternoon sunshine, the vendors setting out their wares, homes where people were beginning to stir after their afternoon rest, the span of sapphire sky overhead. "I put Calcutta into my paintings, and I don't want to replace it with New York."

"Oh. I see. A move like that would change you as a painter."

"It would change me as a person. And I don't want that. Besides, now that you're not going anywhere, painting at home is much more bearable than it used to be."

"I make your life more *bearable*?" she asked, so relieved that he was staying that she couldn't resist the urge to tease him. "Is that the best word you can come up with?"

He smiled back. "Interesting, then. You make my life more interesting. Better?"

"A bit."

They talked about the new painting he was working on, a landscape of their neighborhood. Soon, too soon, Reet called from below, and Asha floated down the stairs.

Her sister met her at the landing. "Him again?" Reet asked.

Asha nodded, and couldn't keep herself from smiling.

"Lucky you," her sister said. "Lucky him."

Asha's smile faded as she registered her sister's narrow silhouette in the hall. "Reet, have you eaten anything today?"

"I had some tea and a couple of biscuits. Don't scold me

all the time, okay? It was hard enough to eat those, and I'm trying my best."

"No rags on the line again this month."

"No washing them, either. Now, hurry; Raj is waiting for you."

# TWENTY-THREE

Raj was sitting with his math book closed, and he didn't let her open it when she reached for it.

"We have to review that problem from yesterday, Raj," Asha said. "You still don't see how—"

"Shut up about the math. I've got something to tell you."

She sat back. "What is it?"

"Ma is . . . she's hammering away at Baba night after night. I've heard them."

"About what?"

"About Reet. She wants Baba to put the word out that we're receiving proposals for real this time."

"And what does your father say?"

"She's wearing him down. We can't have a wedding in the home until a year has passed, but she keeps telling him that it takes a while to arrange a match. Last night he agreed to tell some of his friends."

"Oh no! Listen, Raj, thanks for telling me."

"But what can we do? You can't rip apart *all* your sister's potential husbands on the tennis court."

Asha smiled ruefully. "I know." That prank seemed like child's play now. This time things were serious. She had to talk to Reet. "I'll take care of it. Now let's get back to your math; this exam I want you at the very top of the list."

After they were done, she found her sister and took her into the bathroom to be assured of total privacy. It didn't reek now that Reet had started managing the two servants who still worked for them. In fact, it sparkled, and smelled of lemon juice and vinegar. When the girls hid in there, sometimes one or both of them still cried over Baba, but more and more they talked about how to save their mother.

"Grandmother keeps going on about money," Reet said now. "Ma hates that beyond anything."

"And Auntie's really bossy in the kitchen, have you noticed? She treats Ma like one of the servants."

"What can we do, Osh? How can we help her? We promised Baba we'd take care of her and we're failing. Her heart's like a stone, and nothing I try seems to break through."

"It gets worse."

"What do you mean?"

Asha didn't mince words: "They're going to marry you off, Reet." She told her sister what Raj had overheard.

Reet absorbed the blow quietly. "That might be our only choice, Osh," she said finally. "I can't keep living here forever, sponging off Uncle and Auntie. It will make things easier for Ma if they're spending less on us, and maybe I'd be able to send her some money of her own."

"No, it isn't your only choice, Reet! It can't be! We can . . ."

Asha's voice trailed off; she couldn't think of anything her sister could do to leave the house apart from getting married.

"It would actually be better if I bring it up before Uncle has a chance to," Reet continued. "I've been giving it some thought myself. Listen, if I can find a man with some money, I can take care of Ma *and* you. Maybe you could move in with me."

"I'm one hundred percent certain that your mother-in-law-to-be is not going to want Ma and me lurking around."

"I'll marry a man whose parents are dead, then."

"Oh, *that's* going to be easy. Uncle is going to request proposals only from rich orphans. I'm sure there are three hundred of those in our neighborhood at least."

"No need for sarcasm, Osh," Reet said. "Our relatives can surely find one or two in Calcutta who fit the bill." She paused. "My only hope is that our husbands will be as kind to us as Baba always was to Ma."

"Definitely. Remember that new bride down the street in Delhi who used to drape her saree to hide her bruises?"

Reet leaned over and kissed her sister on the cheek. "We'll be fine, don't worry."

The next day at tea, Reet held Asha's hand tightly under the table and took the plunge. "Uncle, Grandmother, I have something to ask you."

Ma, who was passing around a plate full of steaming samosas, looked quickly at her older daughter.

"Yes, Shona?" Grandmother asked.

"I'm—I'm ready to get married," Reet said.

The plate fell on the floor and shattered. "What?" Ma asked. "Why didn't you talk this over with me first?"

Reet looked confused. "But, Ma. Uncle and Auntie—I mean, you're so . . . I'm sorry, Ma. I'm sorry."

Ma stepped carefully over the pile of crumbled samosas and broken china on the floor as she left the room. The girls exchanged desperate looks, but they knew they couldn't take care of their mother till later.

"I'm glad you brought that up, Shona," Auntie said, smiling. "We think you're ready to be married; you're as old as I was when my parents found your uncle. I'm sure your father would give his blessing."

"And besides, then we'll have one less mouth to feed around here," Raj said disgustedly, standing up and shoving his chair into the table. "That's what you mean; why don't you say it?"

"Beta!" his mother gasped.

Uncle stood up, strode around the table, and grabbed his son by the ear. Gripping tightly, he shook the ear so that Raj's whole body rocked back and forth several times. "A son *never* talks to his mother like that, do you hear me?"

Raj yanked his ear away from his father's hand. "Ow!

Yes, I hear you," he said, and left the room. They could hear him fighting back sobs as he raced upstairs.

"Eesh!" said Grandmother. "Neither of *my* boys ever talked to me like that. A mother has to teach her son how to respect her."

Auntie threw a look of fury at her mother-in-law before making her own exit. They heard the door to her bedroom slam behind her.

"Oh, if only your father and my Bintu were still alive," Grandmother said, starting to cry again and heading to her prayer room.

Sita and Suma got up from the floor and came to the table. "What's the matter, Shonadi?" Suma asked Reet. "Why is everybody crying and fighting and shouting?"

"And leaving?" Sita added.

"It's my fault," Reet said, standing up, too, the tears beginning to fall. "I thought I was trying to help, but I've just made everything worse. I'm sorry, Uncle." And then *she* left the room, followed by the twins, who were doing their best to comfort her.

Uncle and Asha were alone, staring across the table at each other. "So your sister wants to get married?" he asked finally.

"Not really," Asha answered, testing the waters. "But it's her only choice, it seems."

Uncle tipped his head to one side, agreeing, and her heart sank. "What sort of a boy should I look for?" he asked.

"Somebody who will be good to her, Uncle. Just look for that."

"I'll do my best, Tuni. I'll try to find the husbands my brother would have chosen. For both of you girls."

Asha cringed at being included. "Thank you, Uncle. You're very good to us."

They finished their tea in silence; then Asha brought in a broom to clean up the mess her mother had left on the floor.

When Asha went upstairs, Reet was pretending to be asleep under the mosquito net.

"Shhh," Suma told her as the twins tiptoed out of the room. "We stroked Shonadi's hair until she fell asleep."

"Thanks, sweeties," Asha said, feeling a rush of love for her cousins. Even Raj's insolence had been a way of standing up for them.

She crawled in next to her sister. "What do we do now?" she asked.

"We made a big mistake, Osh," Reet said. "We dishonored Ma by not going to her first."

"But what could she do, anyway? It's not her decision. Besides, she's nowhere in sight these days, Reet; the Jailor has taken her over totally. It's been four months now since we heard the news about Baba, and she hasn't cried a single tear."

"We should still treat her as though she's Ma, even if she's not acting like herself."

"She doesn't care enough to even scold us much anymore."

"She spoke up that day we came back from the Ganga. To defend Baba. Remember?"

"That was the last time she said a word to either of us."

"Osh, she's devastated. We're all she has left. We have to keep trying."

Asha sighed. "All right. Let's go."

They walked down the hall hand in hand past Raj's closed door to the small room where their mother slept. "Should we knock?" Reet asked.

"No. Let's barge in like we used to in Delhi."

"You first."

Asha turned the handle and pushed the door open. Their mother was sitting in the small chair by the window and staring into the coconut leaves outside. She didn't turn to greet them; silhouetted against the window in her white saree, she reminded Asha of a faded black-and-white photo.

"Ma?" Reet ventured. "I'm sorry."

"You don't have to be, Shona," Ma answered. "You were right to go to your uncle first. I can't help you anymore."

"Yes, you can, Ma!" Asha said, walking over to where she could see her mother's face. "You have to speak up! They'll marry Reet off to anybody they want!"

"Why should they listen to me? I'm nothing in this house. A dead son's wife's mouth is for feeding, not for speaking."

Asha's hand twitched with a desire to slap the Jailor out of her mother's face. But at least she was talking; they had to keep the words coming. "If you say something about the kind of boy they should choose for Reet, they'll hear it. Talk about what Baba would have wanted; Grandmother has to weigh *that* into the decision."

Reet walked over, squatted in front of Ma, took both of

her mother's hands in hers, and looked up into her face. "Please, Ma?" she asked.

But their mother pulled her hands away. "I can't do anything for you girls," she repeated.

She stood up, went to the door, and waited until the girls left. They could hear her locking the door behind them. Asha and Reet slowly made their way down the hall.

"They're both dead," Asha said. "We're orphans."

"No! Osh, don't say that. We can get her back. I know we can."

"Only Baba could do that, and he's gone, Reet. It's up to us, but I'm at my wits' end."

"What about knitting? Maybe we can get her some wool."

"How? We can't afford it."

"That's the first thing I'll buy with my husband's money," Reet declared. "A skein of the best-quality wool in Calcutta. And then you'll have to make sure she uses it."

"She'll be knitting baby booties someday," Asha said, trying to smile.

"Disgusting thought," Reet answered. "I plan to wait a few months after the wedding like Grandmother until we get to know each other."

"What if the kind, rich orphan boy doesn't want to wait?"

"He'll have to," Reet said. "Now get downstairs with the twins and start making yourself indispensable."

# TWENTY-FOUR

"It's 1975 tomorrow," Asha told Jay one afternoon. She was up on the roof wrapped in a wool shawl. The days were colder, and on some afternoons, she could see their breath in the air as they talked.

"I know. Big celebrations in other parts of the world."

"Except here. People in Calcutta still don't pay much attention to the Western calendar."

"Nobody seems to be paying attention to news outside our borders. Prime Minister Gandhi is bound to be overthrown by the opposition—they're getting more powerful every day."

"I know. Uncle has the radio on every minute. But she'll fight back, don't worry."

"And we'll have to pay the price," he said.

"What do you mean?" she asked.

"Our freedom. We'll have to give that up if Mrs. Gandhi tries to get things under her control. Soldiers on the streets. The newspapers not able to write anything against the government. No elections. Curfews."

"Probably won't change my life one bit," Asha said. "What difference does a curfew make when you're already not allowed to go out?"

Since Baba had died, she and her sister had left the house only once—to sprinkle his ashes over the river. Ma hadn't stepped outside the gate at all. Sometimes Asha thought that if it hadn't been for Reet, and teaching her cousins, and the time she spent with Jay, the boredom of her days would have sent her running into the Jailor's arms.

"I hear you're working miracles with your cousins' schoolwork," Jay said.

"Who told you?"

"Oh, your aunt bragged about their results to my mother, who immediately told my aunt, who told her neighbor. Which means—you're about to get a job offer."

"I am?"

"Yes. My aunt's neighbor's daughter is apparently quite stupid. The neighbor wants you to start tutoring, and he's going to offer you five rupees an hour."

"He is? Jay, that's great news!"

Asha started dancing around the roof, her ankle bracelets sounding like tambourines, hair floating around her like a veil. It had grown out to her shoulders; she always wore it loose when she came up to talk to Jay. After a few more spins, she stopped to catch her breath. "Why didn't you tell me right away? You know how much I want to earn some money!"

"I didn't want to get your hopes up," he said. "I wasn't sure if it was really going to happen. But here comes your potential employer now; I see him rounding the corner. Run downstairs and make a good impression."

Asha stopped in her room to comb and braid her hair and take off her ankle bracelets. She paused just outside the living room to make sure the scarf of her salwar was draped properly around her shoulders, and peeked in. Ma was nowhere in sight, and neither was Grandmother, but Uncle was smiling agreeably, Auntie was beaming, and Reet was serving tea.

"It will be a good chance for our brilliant niece," Auntie was saying. "She was born to be a teacher."

Their guest was a meek-looking plump man. "Why not let her study, then?" he asked curiously. "Our city has several wonderful teachers' colleges for young women."

Auntie and Uncle exchanged careful glances. "She... er... isn't quite ready to study so soon after her father's death."

Tuition at the colleges was steep; Asha had no hope of ever attending. Besides, she wanted to be a psychologist, not a teacher. Anybody could be a teacher, but as far as she knew, there wasn't another Bengali woman psychologist around and there definitely needed to be. How she was going to make her dream come true, she had no idea, but earning some money was definitely the first step. Taking a deep breath, she walked into the room.

"Ah, here's my niece," Uncle said, gathering himself up to make the necessary introductions.

Suddenly someone pushed past Asha like a whirlwind. It was Grandmother. "What's this? What's this? The little girls told me somebody was trying to hire our Tuni to do some work in their house for them. Is this true?"

Their guest rose courteously. "Yes, madam, I am. I've heard she's making real strides with your granddaughters' studies. My daughter needs a tutor, and—"

Grandmother drew herself up to her full height, which was about as high as Asha's shoulder. She held up one palm in front of the gentleman's face. "You will find your tutor somewhere else, sir. My husband was a highly educated man, and my own father was a landowner. Any grandchildren living under *my* roof will earn salaries as professionals, not an hourly wage as hired help."

The guest backed toward the door, stuttering and stumbling as he went. "I'm sorry, I'm sorry. Pardon me, I was misinformed. Thank you, I'm sorry." He was gone, and with him Asha's chances of earning a single rupee.

"Grandmother! What's so degrading about earning money?" she demanded, ignoring the warning look Reet flashed her way.

"Being a teacher is a fine job," Auntie added. "And we could have used the extra money."

*I wasn't going to give it to YOU,* Asha thought angrily, but she didn't say it aloud. What was the point of arguing over hypothetical earnings? Nobody could use them now.

"Becoming a schoolteacher would be fine," Grandmother said sternly. "But sending an unmarried girl of our class and caste to work in someone else's home is another. What were you thinking, Bontu? Your brother would never have allowed this."

Ma came in. "What's going on?" she asked.

"*They* almost agreed to hire your daughter out as a tutor," Grandmother answered, tilting her head toward Auntie and Uncle. "Thankfully, I stopped them."

Ma looked at Asha, who was still glowering, fists clenched by her sides. "Why can't she take the job? She's quite good at helping others with their studies."

"I'm not having the neighbors accuse us of taking advantage of my son's family," Grandmother said haughtily. "What would they think if I sent Tuni out to work so soon after his death?"

"That we need money!" Asha said, trying not to shout. "What's wrong with that?"

"You are not bringing any more shame into this house, young lady," Grandmother said, wagging a finger in Asha's face. "If your father had known about your cutting of hair and playing that game in public with a bunch of boys, he would have had a heart attack."

"No, Baba would have laughed," she retorted. "Baba would have asked me what shots I used to clinch the match."

"That's enough, Tuni," Uncle said sternly.

Reet flashed her sister a frightened look, but Asha couldn't stop herself. She was too frustrated at losing the job. "Are you going to pull *my* ear now, Uncle? Well, go ahead, but no matter how hard you try, you are *not* my father and you never will be!" She spun around and ran upstairs, leaving behind a stunned silence.

Up, up, and up to the roof she raced, where Jay would be, waiting to listen, comfort, sympathize, talk. Sure enough, he leaned out the window. "What happened? Got the job that fast?"

"No, Jay. Grandmother won't let me work outside the home."

"Why not?"

"Something about 'our class' and 'our caste' and earning money as hired help. I don't know! It's so maddening. What am I going to do?"

"If I had my way, Osh, I'd help you get enrolled in the best psychology program in the world. I'd take care of your mother and sister. And you."

Asha caught her breath. His voice was so tender. "Thank you, Jay," she managed. "But it's hard to get your way in this world."

"But we can try, can't we?"

She had to smile at that. "We can always try," she said.

# TWENTY-FIVE

THAT NIGHT, WITH THE TWO OF THEM LOCKED INSIDE THE bathroom while they brushed their teeth, Reet filled Asha in on what had happened in the living room after her exit. "They blamed Ma, of course," Reet said. "Pass the toothpaste."

"Oh no! What did Ma say?" Asha handed her sister the tube of Colgate.

Reet brushed her teeth, rinsed, and spit before answering. "Nothing. All three of them scolded her about what a terrible job she'd done raising you, and she just sat there and took it."

Asha's jubilation over Jay dissipated; she felt crushed. "I made things worse for her, Reet," she said, putting toothpaste on her own brush. "I never should have spoken to Uncle like that. Or to Grandmother. What should I do?"

"Swallow your pride and ask for forgiveness. From Uncle *and* Grandmother. For Ma's sake."

"But that job! I almost had it, Reet." Asha started brushing her teeth. Hard.

"Ma doesn't need us to make things worse for her in this house, Osh. We have to be the two best-behaved, most well-bred girls in Calcutta. Which reminds me, be careful up on the roof. I caught Suma and Sita in the nick of time this afternoon. They were skipping up there because they heard you. Getting caught would be the end of your reputation, Osh. Not to mention Ma's."

Asha shuddered as she rinsed and spit. How terrible if she and Jay were discovered! That could never happen. They'd have to be even more careful than they already were, meeting once a week, maybe, instead of three or four times. But being with him had become an addiction; she wasn't sure she could cut back.

She did take her sister's advice about the apologies, though. Using her best flowery, formal language, she petitioned her uncle and grandmother for forgiveness and understanding because obviously grief had deranged her. And she knew how badly their mother felt over her rudeness, she told everybody. Ma would never permit such behavior from one of her daughters.

Ma sat quietly in the corner and didn't say anything, but Grandmother dropped a kiss on her granddaughter's forehead. "We're all mixed up after losing your father, Tuni," she said. "Especially me."

Uncle sounded weary when he spoke. "I know I can't

take his place, Tuni, but I have to take care of you girls. I'm trying as hard as I can."

Now she felt genuinely sorry. "I know, Uncle."

He smiled and turned to Reet. "We've begun asking for proposals, Shona. Hopefully they'll start coming in soon. We have to wait a few more months for a wedding, but I'm glad you are entrusting me and your grandmother with this decision. I'll find you a good match, don't worry."

"It's getting harder these days to find a decent husband for girls who don't go to college," Auntie added. "But we'll do our best. It's too bad you've lost your figure, Shona. Try to eat something."

It was true. Reet was now skinnier than Asha had ever been. Her cheekbones and jawline were as sharp as the edges of the faces in Howrah station. There was no longer a group of idiots gathering on the corner to try and glimpse Reet's figure; there was hardly anything left to ogle. She'd not had her period again, and Asha was getting more and more concerned. The list of worries she couldn't do a thing about was growing.

Ma came up to their room that night for the first time in months, carrying a steaming bowl of rice and lentils. "Shona, I've made you some fresh supper," she said, using her sweet-sounding village Bangla again. To Asha's ears, it sounded like a flute in perfect tune. "Sometimes it's easier to eat without the family around shouting and gossiping. Tuni, tell a story to your sister while she eats. Like your baba used to."

Asha remembered with a jolt that when they were little girls, Reet would negotiate a story from Baba in exchange for a plate-cleaning finish to a meal.

The twins were already tucked into bed, but they were still awake. "Yes! Yes!" they shouted. "A story! We want a Tuntuni story!" Asha still read fairy tales to the family, but she hadn't told a Tuntuni story since the telegram.

Asha turned to her sister, who had been combing out her tangles. "Will you eat if I tell it?" she asked.

"I'll try," Reet said.

"I've made the dal just like my mother used to," Ma said, and Asha noted the rare reference to one of the Strangers.

Ma kissed her older daughter on the cheek. It was the first time she'd done that to either girl since they'd arrived in Calcutta, and Asha felt a pang as she watched. "Your uncle will take care of you, Shona," Ma said. "May he find a husband for you as good as your baba."

Then she leaned down and kissed Asha, too. After she left, the girls smiled at each other through their tears.

"Start eating, Reet," Asha commanded, and she began a Tuntuni story that she stretched out, just as Baba used to, until her sister finished every bite.

# TWENTY-SIX

THE LATE-NIGHT SUPPER, HANDMADE AND HAND-DELIVERED, turned into a ritual, as did the good-night kisses from Ma and a story from Asha. After a few weeks of this special treatment, Reet looked healthier, and soon her rags were drying beside her sister's in the side garden. The side that was farthest from Jay's house, for which Asha was grateful.

"It's strange how girls start to bleed together," Asha said as they pegged their washed cloths to the line. "At Bishop, a lot of us got our period at the same time, remember?"

"So that's why the bathroom got jammed three days a month!"

The girls laughed and picked up their empty buckets. They stopped by the pump, and Reet was about to start rinsing out her bucket.

"Shhh," Asha warned suddenly.

Voices were arguing in the kitchen—Auntie's and Grandmother's. And Ma's. Hardly believing that their mother could be participating so vigorously in a discussion, the girls listened through the open door.

"We simply cannot accept that one," Ma said.

"There is no other proposal, Sumitra. She used to have her looks, at least, but now those are gone." That was Auntie, of course.

"But this widower in Madras," Grandmother said. "How old is he?"

"Not much over twenty-seven or -eight, I'm sure," Auntie answered. "And he's a chemistry professor, like Bontu's father used to be."

"Oh, lovely," said Grandmother.

"And his family?" Ma asked.

"His mother's a widow, like you. She has an older son who's already married, and they have one boy, but the other daughter-in-law is sickly. They want the unmarried son to find a wife who is 'young and healthy,' the ad said, so I'm assuming they need help managing the nephew."

"So my Shona would have to work hard," Ma said. "I don't like the sound of that."

"Nothing wrong with hard work," Auntie said.

*Easy for you to say,* Asha thought. *Ma and Reet do most of it around here.*

"And what do the stars say?" Grandmother asked.

"Good news. The astrologer predicts a harmonious match. Their family is of good caste and education, Ma. He's perfect for Shona."

"Don't you read the newspapers?" Ma's voice sounded like her old self, sharp and strong. "High-caste, educated husbands do terrible things to their brides, too. That's why we should find boys in Calcutta, so we can ask questions here and there and find out what we need to know."

"It's not as if she has other choices," Auntie said. "It's already been two months since we started asking around, and this is her only proposal, Sumitra."

"Why aren't more coming?" Grandmother asked. "We're a good family. And she's still a lovely girl. Plenty of boys these days don't require a large dowry, or any at all. What about that Mitra fellow who wanted to marry her some time back?"

"He won't have anything to do with her. Apparently . . ." Auntie hesitated. "There's some terrible gossip going around town. I only hope it doesn't get to Madras before the marriage is fixed."

"Gossip?" Ma asked quickly. "About us?"

"About the train 'accident.' "

"If you mean that people are implying it wasn't an accident, then say that, please. I can't afford to play games. This is my daughter's future we're talking about."

"All right, then. That's what they're saying. That the girls' father was mentally unstable, gave up, took his own life."

Reet grabbed Asha's salwar to restrain her. "Ma's handling it," she hissed, and Asha subsided.

"My husband died *accidentally*." Ma's voice wasn't loud, but it was so full of anger that Asha felt like applauding. This was their mother in full glory with no sign of the Jailor, at least for now.

"Well, nobody around here wants to risk bringing that kind of instability into their family line," Auntie said. "I'm afraid it's going to hinder my own daughters' chances when the time comes for them to receive proposals."

Grandmother spoke up. "If we start acting as if something else might be true, we'll end up feeding this terrible gossip instead of stopping it. Let's wait awhile before accepting this proposal. Maybe something else will arrive for our Shona. In the meantime, hold your head high, Sumitra. My son was a good man. He would never have done that to us."

"I know, I know. Now, where are those daughters of mine?"

Hurriedly, the girls grabbed their buckets and backed away from the door. When their mother came out to find them, they tried their best to seem as though they were just strolling up the garden path.

Ma scanned their faces. "Did you hear our conversation?" she asked.

"What conversation?" Asha asked.

"We were washing our rags, Ma," Reet added.

"I hope so," Ma said sternly. "Now come inside and stir this paneer while I run to the bathroom and change my own cloth. It's my time, too, believe it or not."

Asha stayed in the kitchen while her sister stirred. "What do you think?"

Reet shrugged. "At least Ma sounded like herself. That's good."

"Yes, but what about Mr. Madras with the sickly sister-in-law?"

Reet handed her sister the wooden spoon and reached for the peas. "Here, you stir. I'll shell these. Listen, I have to trust Uncle. He and Grandmother and Ma will make the right choice for me. What else can I do? Everything Auntie said is true—except for the part about Baba, of course. A girl like me doesn't get to pick and choose."

Asha scooped and turned the paneer so it wouldn't burn. "Well, the good news is that Ma was right there speaking up for you. And Grandmother sounds reasonable, too. Let's hope for the best." She put down the spoon and wiped her hands on a towel.

"Where are you going, Osh?"

"Er . . . up to the roof."

"Not yet, sister of mine. It's only been two days."

"Are you keeping a record now?"

"No, but the little girls are. I've caught them on the roof twice now when you're not there. They're definitely snooping. 'Why does Tunidi come up here so much?' they asked me. 'She likes to write in her diary,' I told them. But you haven't written much lately, have you?"

"No, not much. He's waiting for me, though, Reet. I know it."

"Let him wait. It's good for him."

Asha sighed. "How's *my* story going to end, Reet?"

"I have no idea. Hopefully, we'll both live happily ever after."

*I'm going to make sure we do,* Asha thought as their mother returned to start peeling potatoes.

# TWENTY-SEVEN

No other proposals came for Reet. Ma didn't say anything to her daughters directly, but Asha noticed that their mother made sure Reet was always dressed in a good saree and that she opened the curtains as wide as they could go. Weeks went by, and the girls heard nothing more about the potential husband in Madras. Reet stayed calm, as though she really trusted her uncle and grandmother, but Asha's anxiety grew daily.

"We've been in Calcutta for more than a year now," Asha told her sister one night when the twins were asleep. The hot season was coming again and the ceiling fan whirled overhead; it was easier to talk under the sound of it.

"More than a year since we saw Baba's face," Reet said wistfully. "I'm eighteen now, Osh. My birthday was last month."

"Oh, Reet, I'm sorry. I totally forgot. Of course, we couldn't celebrate it."

"We forgot yours, too, in December. Who cares about birthdays, anyway?"

"I remembered it was mine that evening. And I thought about how Baba always gave me a new diary."

"I'd have gotten you one if I could, Osh. But you haven't written in your old one much, it's probably only half full."

"I know. I'm seventeen, Reet. That sounds so grown up, doesn't it?" She wanted to add: *The proof is that when I'm on the roof, and sense Jay's eyes on me, my whole body aches for him . . .*

Her roof visits were fewer and farther between, and although Jay complained, he understood that they couldn't chance getting caught. Besides, lately he was missing again, cloistered in the servants' quarters, immersed once more in finishing a painting. This time he'd told Asha before disappearing, which she'd appreciated.

"Ma seems a bit better these days," Reet said. "Don't you think?"

"A bit. But she hates it here so much."

"Maybe Mr. Madras will let you move in with me."

"Sounds like he's got a mother of his own," Asha answered. "And a brother with a wife and a son. They won't want two more stomachs to fill."

"If he's as rich as Auntie made him sound . . ."

"I doubt it. Anyway, rich people can be stingier than anybody. We have no idea what this man is really like, Reet."

"Uncle said he'll travel there to meet them before arranging the marriage. He'll do the right thing, Osh."

"I wish I could go with him," Asha said. "Hey, maybe Raj could go."

"That's a great idea! We'll ask him to be our spy. We can definitely trust good old Raj."

When his cousins asked him to accompany his father on a fact-finding mission to Madras, Raj agreed immediately. "You can be sure I'll go. I'll get the true story about this fellow, don't you worry."

Asha felt better after that. She did trust Raj; he had proved himself more than once.

One night after dinner, Uncle did that throat-clearing thing that Asha had come to recognize. It meant he wanted to talk about something big.

"No other proposals have come in for Shona," he announced. "And this man in Madras is growing tired of waiting for our answer. What should I tell him?"

"Is it time to take a trip and meet him?" Grandmother suggested.

"Train tickets cost money," Auntie said. "We should accept the proposal first. Then maybe *he'll* send the ticket."

"What?" Ma asked. "Accept the proposal sight unseen? We can't do that. The girls' father would certainly never have acted in such a careless manner."

Grandmother tilted her head in agreement. "She's right. Bintu wouldn't have done that."

"So what do we do?" Auntie asked. "It's not as if she's got other choices. And believe me, we've tried hard to get another proposal, but nobody seems interested."

"Okay, then," Uncle said, sighing. "I'll take a trip to Madras and meet the man face to face."

Auntie looked grim. "Maybe he'll reimburse the ticket if you agree to the match."

"Maybe," Uncle said. "But I have to meet him first. It's what my brother would have done."

"Baba, can I join you on the trip?" Raj asked.

"No, Beta, we certainly don't have money for two tickets," Auntie said.

"I've got some money of my own saved up—gifts from *your* parents, Ma," he said. "I'd like to use it for this."

"What? Why?"

"Oh, I don't know. I've never seen Madras, and I've been studying so hard, it might be nice to take a trip with Baba."

Uncle looked pleased. "I'd enjoy your company, in fact," he said. "And your marks have been top-notch. Okay, it's settled, then. I'll book two tickets to Madras tomorrow and we'll go over the weekend."

Asha leaned closer to her cousin and whispered, "I'll pay you back."

"No, you won't," Raj answered in a low voice. "I'm dying to see the man with my own eyes. I'm happy to pay such a low price for a treat like that."

While Uncle and Raj were gone that weekend, Asha risked a trip up to the roof, but there was no sign of Jay. Instead Suma and Sita finally discovered her.

"Tunidi!" they cried as they rushed through the door. "We found you!"

"Where's your diary?" asked Suma.

"We want to read it!" said Sita.

Asha tried hard not to let the dismay show on her face. "I just came up for some air, girls. Now, come down with me. The walls are low up here, and it's time to do schoolwork." *Thank goodness Jay wasn't there,* she thought. *I'd have a lot of explaining to do about the fairy tale I've been living.*

⁂

After three long days, Raj and his father returned from their trip just in time for dinner.

"How was he?" Grandmother asked eagerly after they'd washed their hands and feet and settled down to eat. "Is he a good match?"

"He seemed like it to me," Uncle said. "Tall, fair, well educated, well-spoken. Not exactly handsome, perhaps, but then neither was I."

Auntie smiled. "*I* thought you were handsome," she said.

"You were very handsome," Grandmother said. "Both my boys were." She wiped a tear from her cheek with the end of her saree.

Asha took stock of her cousin's expression. Why was Raj frowning?

"But about this boy in Madras," Ma said. "Will he make a good husband for Shona?"

"The charts match them up nicely," Uncle said. "The university people spoke highly of him, and the neighbors told me he was quiet and kept to himself. That's good, right?"

"That's excellent," Auntie said. "A man who's a

busybody is just as bad as a woman who gossips. If not worse. What about the house?"

"It wasn't as big as I'd hoped, a bit smaller than ours, but it was clean."

"What did you think, Raj?" Asha asked.

"I already told Baba what I think," Raj said. "Will you tell them, Baba, or shall I?"

"Oh, that small thing. That's nothing for your aunt and cousins to worry about. The boy thinks he knows more than the stars."

"We should know everything," Ma said, turning to Grandmother. "Every doubt, every question."

Grandmother nodded. "Tell us, Bontu."

Uncle scanned the eagerly listening faces, his own two daughters included. "Oh, we'll tell you later. It's nothing, anyway. Right now, I'm starving. The hotel we stayed in served dirt instead of food. I've missed this good cooking." He gestured at one of Ma's signature dishes, chickpeas and potatoes, which he obviously loved, since he always took four helpings.

The girls didn't get to talk to Raj alone until after the twins were asleep and they visited his room. "So what's wrong with him?" Asha demanded.

"He won't do," Raj said immediately. "His six-year-old nephew didn't say a word to him for three days, and the kid seemed *scared*."

"Maybe the boy's just shy," Reet said.

"He's not, though. He talked to everybody else. Chattered away, in fact. I took him out to the garden to play catch, and he babbled on nonstop."

"Did you get anything out of him?" Asha asked.

"I tried the second afternoon, but the kid looked absolutely terrified when I brought the subject up. 'Tell me why you're scared of your uncle,' I said in as kind a voice as I could, and I offered him sweets and everything, but he dashed into the house. Never spoke to me again. I told Baba, but he thinks the kid could be retarded or something. But he wasn't; he was a nice, smart boy—until I started questioning him about his uncle."

"So why *was* he so scared, then?" Asha asked.

"That's what I'm wondering," Raj said.

"Thanks, Raj, for telling us, but a six-year-old's opinion isn't going to shut the door to this marriage," Reet said.

"Couldn't we find out more?" Asha asked.

"Why should we?" Raj demanded. "I don't trust the man one bit. Turn him down, I told Baba."

"But . . . but there's nobody else," Reet said, her voice getting smaller with each word until they could barely hear the last one.

"Just wait, then. Someone is sure to come along." Raj took each of their hands in his, something he'd never done before. "In the meantime, I'll try to talk to Baba again."

But Raj's doubts obviously weren't strong enough, because the next day Uncle announced that he'd accepted the proposal. The match was made. Reet was to marry Dr. Poritosh Ghosh of Madras just after the year marker of Baba's death.

# TWENTY-EIGHT

ASHA WROTE IN HER DIARY THAT NIGHT, LOCKING HERSELF IN the bathroom. She was afraid to venture onto the roof, even though Jay was nowhere in sight. She missed him fiercely.

*I promised Baba I'd take care of Reet. I promised. Maybe this man in Madras would turn out to be a good husband, but maybe not. How could I live with myself if he was horrible to my sister and I could have stopped it? I've got to be sure she marries someone who will treat her as she deserves.*

*But, S.K., what can I do? I only know one other person who might marry her, and he's . . . someone I love. Someone I want. And he loves me. I know he does. ME, S.K. Not like the rest of them, dazzled by the usual stuff. How could I ever give that up? I can't.*

*But I promised Baba I'd take care of Reet. I promised.*

She wrote the same circle of thought again and again in the next few days, not sleeping, barely eating, avoiding conversation with everybody as much as she could. Reet was locked in her own trance, obviously trying to accept the inevitable. At night, though, the sisters still curled together, seeking wordless comfort from each other's presence.

The real Ma was making tentative reappearances here and there, standing up for Reet when it came to things like setting a date or negotiating the dowry that the family in Madras wanted. Otherwise, she still seemed in the grip of the Jailor.

"Do you think she'll return for the wedding?" Reet asked. "I want her to be happy, Osh."

"I don't think she'll be happy until she knows you're safe," Asha said. "And neither will I."

But how could they be sure? Once a girl was married, there was no way for her to escape. Heading repeatedly into the bathroom with her diary, Asha realized that Ma was asking the same anxious questions.

Soon, Asha knew she was running out of time. The date of the wedding was about to be set by the astrologer, relatives informed, invitations ordered. One afternoon, she slowly climbed up to the roof. Jay had to be there, he had to. She brought her diary with her just in case, and when his window stayed closed she collapsed in her old corner and started to write yet again.

*I've made my decision, S.K. I have to ask him. I don't really have a choice. Will he agree? Do I want him to? Oh, S.K., I don't know what to do. I can't let Reet marry this Ghosh fellow, I just can't. I promised Baba I'd take care of Reet. But what if he doesn't want to do it? He has to! I won't give him a choice. And what about Reet? What will she think? Help me, S.K., help me.*

For once, her diary seemed to answer, and the shutters across the way flew open. "Good news, Osh!" Jay called. "I finished it. It's not as good as the other one was, but I sent it to the same gallery."

"Did they sell the first one?"

"They've gotten a lot of offers, but nothing that seemed right to me."

"No good offers?"

"Let's say your face is worth more than the value of a new Mercedes-Benz."

"What's that?"

"A fancy car they sell in Europe. We'll get one when I take you there and I'll teach you to drive it. Did you know I can drive?"

She forced herself to smile. "I believe it. You can do anything, Jay."

"Oh no, Osh. You're never that direct with your compliments. I usually have to tease them out of you. What's the matter?"

Asha took a deep breath. With his curly hair and kind smile, and the way he'd shaved before coming to see her so that the skin on his cheeks and chin was clean and smooth, he was perfect. But not hers. Never hers.

"Jay, remember when you said you'd do anything for me?"

"Of course I do. And I meant it. You need money? Want me to pummel someone? Just name it, Osh."

Her heart gave one last familiar thump-thump. Asha wondered if it would ever beat again after she said the next three words, words she could never take back: "Marry my sister."

Jay was quiet. "What?" he asked.

"You have to marry Reet, Jay. Please. I have to be sure she's taken care of, that nobody will hurt her. I promised my father." Slowly, painfully, she explained Reet's proposal and the unknowns that were waiting for her in Madras.

"But how do you know she won't be happy with him?" Jay asked.

"I don't know that she would be. Or that he'll be good to her. And I need to be certain that she'll be treated kindly, Jay."

He was quiet again, and then she saw anger on his face for the first time. "You're asking me to propose to your sister." It was a statement, not a question.

"Yes, Jay, I am."

"No, Asha," he said quietly. "I can't do it. That's the one thing I can't do for you."

"You said anything."

"I didn't mean *that.* Why can't I come for *you* instead?" he said. "Then we could take care of Reet and your mother together."

Asha shook her head. "A younger sister marrying first? That never happens, Jay, you know that. At least not in our circles. People will think something's wrong with Reet."

Nobody spoke for a long minute or two.

"Take some time to think about it," she said finally. And then she made the decision as easy for him as she could. "But . . . I don't want to see you again. Not up here. Not like this. The next time we'll meet, Jay, is when and if you're in the house with a marriage proposal for my sister." With an immense effort, she forced herself to turn and leave.

"Asha, wait! Please, wait!" His voice was frantic and loud; he obviously didn't care who heard him. "Asha!"

She ran for the stairs, opened the door, escaped, and shut the door tightly behind her. Then she leaned against it and cried as she hadn't in weeks. After the storm of tears subsided, she washed her face, dried it, and headed straight for Raj's room.

"I need a big padlock," she told him.

"Why?"

"I want to lock the roof. The little girls went up there and it's not safe for them. The walls are too low."

"There's one in the storage room. I'll get it." When he handed it to her, he smiled knowingly. "You'll keep the key, right?"

"What do you mean?" she asked, leading the way upstairs. She looped the big padlock through the latch on the door to the roof and locked it. Then she checked it to make sure it was secure.

"Oh, come on, Osh, I'm not an idiot. I've kept Suma and Sita from running up to interrupt your conversations at least five or six times."

"Well, you don't know everything," she said, leading him downstairs again to the small balcony attached to his room.

"Osh, don't!" he shouted, but it was too late.

She'd hurled the key as far as she could. Her throwing arm was still good; the key landed far on the other side of the trees, somewhere short of the pond.

"Why did you do that?" Raj asked. "Now we'll have to cut the lock the next time someone wants to go up there."

"Exactly," she said, and went to find her sister.

# TWENTY-NINE

Asha didn't tell Reet what she'd done and later wondered if it might have changed the way things turned out. But she kept the secret from her sister, and their lives would never be the same.

Sometimes, while she taught the cousins, or listened to her sister sing, or helped her mother clear the dinner table, she wondered what Jay would decide. She wondered how it would be to love and hate someone at the same time, as he probably loved and hated her. *But I do know how that is,* she thought. *I feel that for myself.*

On the day when Uncle came home early to tea with a big smile on his face, Asha knew what he was about to say.

"We have another proposal for our girl," he announced jubilantly.

"What?"

"Who?"

"When?"

Grandmother, Auntie, and Ma stood stock-still in different corners of the room, waiting for the rest of his news.

"From the young man who lives next door."

Again, they all spoke at once.

"The Crazy One?" That was Grandmother.

"That rich family?" Auntie.

"I knew something better would come!" Ma exulted.

Raj was staring at Asha, his mouth open.

"The stars show an even better match for her with this fellow than the other one," Uncle said.

"For which girl?" Reet's question got their attention.

"For you, of course, darling," Ma said. "What did you think? You're the older girl of the family. You have to be married first."

Reet shook her head. "Oh. But I can't marry *him*."

"Why not?" At least three voices asked the question.

"Is it because he's odd?" Grandmother asked. "I'm a bit worried about that myself."

"No, it's because he doesn't love me."

"Oh, don't worry about that, my dear," Auntie said. "He'll come to love you. All husbands do."

"How could he love you before he marries you?" Grandmother was completely astonished by the question. "He doesn't even know you yet."

"And as for him being strange, why, it's simply not true," Uncle said. "Turns out he's a brilliant painter. Shows his work in a famous gallery in Delhi. He's getting magnificent prices for his paintings, and apparently the one he's just finished is superb. Plus he's been offered a prestigious fellowship in New York, at a university, that could lead to a satisfying teaching career as a fine arts professor if he takes it."

"And why wouldn't he take it?" Ma asked. "To think of my Reet getting another chance to go to New York! Why, it's as if . . . as if my beloved is making this all happen."

And for the second time in their lives, the girls watched their mother begin to cry. As Reet and Asha both rushed to her side, their eyes met. "Let it be," Asha whispered. "Please, Reet."

"For now," Reet answered, as she gathered Ma in her arms just as she had on the train.

Ma cried, and cried, and cried, and after a while, Grandmother joined in, and even Uncle wiped away a tear or two. Soon Suma and Sita started sobbing also, even though they had no idea what was going on, and finally Raj led his sisters upstairs.

"So . . ." When Ma's sobs had subsided into hiccups, Uncle cleared his throat again. "Should I accept this proposal, Sumitra? What do the rest of you think?"

Auntie nodded with a trace of envy in her face. "I thought that boy didn't like girls. But he's the only son, and if the stars point to a better match than with the one in Madras, who am I to say we shouldn't turn down the first proposal and accept this one?"

"She'll have good in-laws," Grandmother said. "I've always thought they were fine people."

"Yes, yes, yes," Ma said, delight all over her face. "Why, she'll be right next door!"

"Not if she goes to America," said Auntie.

"But she'll come home to have her babies, and to visit. Oh, it's perfect. Thank you, dear ones, thank you!" Ma began to laugh and cry at the same time, and Reet and Asha held her even more tightly.

"This one's much better than that Ghosh fellow; I wasn't too sure about him, to tell the truth," Uncle said.

Asha released her mother and stood up to face her Uncle. "Then why did we accept the proposal?"

"It was a mistake," Uncle admitted. "I can see it now. Bintu would be delighted with this match. He always loved art; I remember him standing for hours in front of a painting or two at the National Gallery in Delhi when we visited as boys. So it's a go, then?"

"Wonderful!" crowed Grandmother. "I must thank the gods." She left immediately for the prayer room.

"I can't wait to tell my friends," said Auntie. "They'll be so jealous. When can we have the formal meeting? I always love seeing a couple's eyes meet for the first time."

Reet let go of their mother, too. "May I be excused, Uncle?"

"Certainly, Shona. I know you want to think about this in private. I'm so happy for you. I told you I'd take care of you, didn't I?"

"You did. Come, Asha. Let's go."

Asha followed her sister upstairs, dreading this confrontation even more than she had her conversation with Jay.

"Explain," Reet commanded as soon as they were in the

bathroom. She turned the water on full force so nobody could overhear them.

"He wants to marry you," Asha said, glancing quickly at the mirror to see if her secret was revealed in her reflection.

But her sister saw right through her mask of calm control. "No. He wants to marry you. I won't do it, Asha."

"It's too late. You have to. You saw Ma's face. She cried for the first time, Reet."

Reet was silent. Then she punched the wall as hard as she could. "Ow!" She bent over her fist, cradling it with the other hand. Asha reached over to help. "Get back," her sister said. "Don't touch me. I hate you, Asha Gupta."

"Don't say that. This is the perfect solution. And you're perfect for each other."

"Don't lie to me! You adore him, and he must care just as much about you. Why else would he agree to this stupid plan? Oh, how could you do this to me? I thought you loved me." Reet's face crumpled. "Get out. Get out of here." She threw open the door and shoved her sister so hard that Asha almost fell backward into the hall.

Asha banged on the closed door. "I promised Baba I'd take care of you!"

No answer from inside.

"He'll be a brother to me, Reet. I promise. Didn't you see the lock I put on the door a couple of weeks ago?"

No answer.

Raj came out of his room. "Shut *up,* Osh. Do you want the entire world to figure out what happened?"

"She hates me, Raj."

"She'll get over it."

"I doubt it."

"Come in here," he said, leading the way into his room.

"Did I do the right thing?" she asked, flopping onto the floor in a heap.

"What else could you do? I tried my best to get another proposal for Reet around here, Osh. I even went to that first idiot you trounced on the court and begged him to ask again, but he just laughed. Oh, he enjoyed seeing me grovel after what we put him through."

"You did that? For us?"

"None of my friends are old enough to get married yet, although four or five of them volunteered for the position. They think your sister's . . . well, she's still pretty enough, even after what she's been through."

"I hate that a boy is supposed to be six or seven years older than the girl before they can be matched. Who started that stupid tradition?"

"I have no idea."

"Well, the two of us can't change some customs no matter how hard we try," Asha said sadly.

For the first time in their lives, the sisters didn't speak before they went to sleep. Reet's body was as stiff as a fence beside Asha's. Once, Asha tried to touch her sister's shoulder, but Reet jerked back so harshly that it felt as if Asha's fingers were covered with splinters.

# THIRTY

Nobody but Raj noticed the cold war between the Gupta girls. Not only was the house abuzz with the new proposal, but events outside the walls were also changing fast. The prime minister was in trouble, accused of fraud, and Uncle's radio blared news about the possibility of her being overthrown by the opposition.

Meanwhile, Auntie, Grandmother, and Ma were in a frenzy of preparation for the upcoming visit from the family next door. Three days. Two days. Tomorrow. Asha tried to prepare herself to see Jay through sisterly eyes. Could she do it? She'd have to; she had no choice.

Reet was going through the motions, but the few times Asha caught her sister looking at her, the expression on Reet's face made Asha's stomach coil like a snail. What had she done? Was she making the biggest mistake of her life? Was she going to lose both Jay and Reet forever?

*S.K., what can I do now? I can't stop it. We have to move forward. He's coming here to ask for my sister's hand. He'll come to love her in time, I know he will. What man in his right mind wouldn't? And he's so irresistible she's bound to love him. But can I bear watching them fall in love, especially from right next door? What's going to happen to me, S.K.? I've kept my sister safe, but what about me? What happens to my happily-ever-after?*

Ma made her wear the green salwar kameez on the day of the meeting, even though Asha resisted. "Why do *I* have to get dressed up, Ma?" she asked.

"This is a special occasion, meeting your Shala for the first time. A brother-in-law and his wife's sister have a special relationship. You can tease him if you like once they're married, Tuni. You'll have a sweet friendship if it goes well; he's supposed to take care of you always. Until you're married, that is."

Asha put the salwar on but left off the ankle bracelets and asked Ma to tie her hair in a short braid instead of leaving it loose. Meanwhile, Reet was wrapping herself in a shimmering blue saree, the same one she'd worn on the train here. Asha noticed that the extra evening meals had brought back enough of her sister's curves to fill out the blouse decently. How could Jay resist her? But while Reet looked beautiful on the outside, her eyes were icy.

"When you serve him tea, Shona, don't look up," Ma warned. "Wait until somebody urges you to do it. Your auntie will probably be the one. Remember that it isn't proper for the girl to look first. Let him have his turn, then you'll get yours."

"All right, Ma," Reet answered.

Ma gathered her oldest daughter in her arms and held her close. "Oh, I'm so proud of you, Shona. How happy your baba would have been on this day! He would have made them so welcome, like family right away. I'm counting on you, Asha, to do your part."

"I'll try, Ma," Asha answered.

"Now, cheer up, girls. Why, what's wrong with the two of you? This is supposed to be a happy day. Shona's not leaving us yet, and when she does, she's going just next door. Imagine how nice that will be. The two of you can see each other every day."

Sita and Suma came dancing in, dressed in identical frilly blue frocks. "They're here!" they crowed. "Oh, Shonadi, you're so pretty!"

"Girls, I'm going down," Ma said. "Come, Asha."

Jay was wearing the same kurta and pajama he'd worn to Baba's memorial, and sat stiffly between his parents on the sofa in the living room. All three stood up when Asha and her mother came in.

Asha noticed that his hair was cut shorter than she'd ever seen it. He didn't look her way.

"Sumitra, Tuni, come say hello to our guests," Uncle said. He introduced Jay's parents first. "You already know Mr. and Mrs. Sen, our good neighbors."

"Namashkar," his parents said, palms together in greeting.

"Namashkar," Ma answered.

Asha bent to give them the expected pronam.

"And this is Jay, their only son. He came to the memorial; you might have seen him there."

Jay gave Ma pronam, still not looking in Asha's direction at all.

"Sit down, sit down," Uncle said, gesturing to the sofa again.

They sat. Asha perched beside her mother on the hard couch in the other corner of the room. Auntie, Grandmother, and the little girls came bustling in, and the whole namashkar-pronam routine repeated itself, one generation bowing to the other like marionettes. Asha tried not to notice how Jay moved, and how his fingers looked when he tugged on the twins' blue hair ribbons, sending them giggling to their father's knees.

"Bring in the tea, Shona," Ma called.

Almost immediately, as though she'd been waiting outside the door, Reet carried in the full tray.

"Ohhhhh!" gasped Jay's mother. "Such a lovely girl. The gods have heard my prayers."

Reet served Mr. Sen some tea, and then Mrs. Sen. Next the tray was lowered before Jay. Asha couldn't help watching as Jay gazed at her sister's downturned face, the way a prospective bridegroom was supposed to. But he looked away quickly, and his eyes flickered for a split second over to where Asha was sitting. Did anybody else notice?

Apparently nobody had. "Look up, Shona, look up," Auntie trilled. "Don't be shy."

Reet looked up, straight into Jay's face, and then she, too, turned to look at Asha, much sooner than she should have. This time, everyone noticed that she hadn't done it right.

Ma tried to cover for her daughter. "It's hard," she said. "She's shy. And she's so close to her sister, you see."

"He's a good boy," Jay's mother told Reet, concern in her voice. "He'll take care of you."

"The people in Delhi tell me he's a genius," Mr. Sen added gruffly. "A genius! Imagine that!"

"Oh, and I'm taking that job in New York," Jay announced. "That is, if my—my bride approves." He looked up at Reet.

"She approves," Reet said.

"Shhh," Ma hissed. "You're not supposed to talk, Shona. We'll discuss this later."

"But we thought you'd start your married life here," Grandmother said. "With all of us around you."

"We can't," Jay answered. "The prime minister is thinking of imposing a state of emergency. We need to leave India and move to New York as soon as possible. It might not be possible once the emergency is declared and the country shuts down."

Uncle cleared his throat. "The boy's right. It's coming,

no doubt about that. We may not be able to move or speak freely. Terrible times are ahead."

"Then we should leave for America right away," Reet said.

"That's what I've been thinking," Jay answered.

"But what about a wedding?" Ma asked, looking dazed.

"We can't wait until the year of mourning is up," Jay said. "We'll have to elope. Now."

*"What?"* At least four voices said it at once.

"My dear boy, a couple only elopes if they don't have their families' blessings," Mr. Sen said. "Both of you have that. You don't need to elope."

"But if the country's closing down in a few weeks, I want to leave for New York before then," Jay said. "I'd like to take my wife with me."

Asha tried not to react. His cool, matter-of-fact demeanor was cutting her like a knife; each word felt as if she were being stabbed.

"I can't let my niece leave our home without a wedding," Uncle said, frowning. "I owe it to my brother."

"You're our only son," Mrs. Sen added. "We have to invite everybody we know to the wedding."

"Ma, people elope in difficult times," Jay said. "Our friends and family will understand."

"Besides, I don't want a wedding anyway." It was Reet again, disobeying Ma's instructions to be quiet. "Not even when the year's up."

"But . . . but . . . ," Uncle sputtered. "I'll pay for it, I told you, Shona. Don't worry about that."

"What will people say?" Auntie asked.

"I don't care what people say," Reet said. "I want to finish this quickly."

The strangeness of her statement silenced everybody except Jay.

"I'm leaving in four days," he said, detonating another bomb as though they weren't already shattered. "My ticket's booked. We'll have to be married quickly at the temple if this is going to happen at all. I'll get a ticket for Reet before I leave and she can join me as soon as possible."

His parents looked as if they were about to faint, and Asha's own head was spinning. They were getting married this week! Jay was leaving and taking her sister with him. She couldn't say anything; she was having a hard time breathing.

"When did you decide this, Beta?" his father asked. "Why didn't you tell us before?"

"I wanted to meet my bride first, and see if she agreed."

"I agree," Reet said immediately. "What day and time?"

"I'll send a rickshaw for you on Saturday," he said. Then he looked around the room, his eyes scanning every face except one. "Thank you all for understanding. Perhaps we can celebrate when we return for a visit next year. Now if you'll excuse me, I have a lot to do to get ready."

He bent to give a farewell pronam to Auntie, Uncle, Ma, and Grandmother, then left the house without another glance in either Reet's or Asha's direction.

"I'll take these into the kitchen," Reet said, gathering up the still-full teacups and disappearing also.

Jay's parents were talking at once, trying to make excuses for their son's behavior, and Asha's family was doing the same for Reet. The first meeting of bride and groom had been so jarring that everybody was embarrassed.

After their guests left, Uncle slumped in his chair. "An elopement at the temple? With no marriage ceremony or celebrations in our homes? I don't understand this, and I'm not sure Bintu would have liked it one bit. That boy still seems odd to me. Are you sure about him, Sumitra?"

"I loved him," Ma said right away. "He'll never lie to her. And he'll be loyal, too. I can tell. I'm sad they'll be living so far away, but somehow it seems right for at least one of us to start a new life in America."

*He's loyal, all right, Ma,* Asha thought as she wearily trudged upstairs. *He keeps his promises, just as I do.*

# THIRTY-ONE

AGAIN AND AGAIN SHE WENT OVER HER CHOICE IN HER MIND, but she couldn't see how to make it turn out differently. Again and again she saw herself up on the roof, making her request to Jay. His fury. The proposal. Ma's delight. Her sister's cold anger. Their decision to marry quickly and move to New York. It couldn't have ended differently. It was the only way she could have kept her promise to Baba. At least Ma was acting more like herself again, and Reet—well, Reet and Jay would be fine once she, Asha, was no longer around.

*It's like a fairy tale without a happy ending for any of the characters,* she thought as she read "Cinderella" to her cousins. Reet was already in bed, her back to her sister.

"And they lived happily ever after," Asha finished.

"What a lie," said Reet.

"What?" Suma asked. "What do you mean, Shonadi?"

"I mean that life isn't like a story," Reet answered.

"For you it is," Sita said. "You're the princess and Jay is the prince."

*That makes me the wicked stepsister,* Asha thought, tucking the little girls into bed.

꧁꧂

Early Saturday morning, Uncle took Reet to the temple to be married. A few hours later, Reet returned to the Gupta household, even though she was supposed to move under her in-laws' roof. Dutifully, Reet had offered to shift next door, but the Sens insisted she remain where she was until her departure as a gift to Ma.

Now Asha heard her sister making the girls' bed as she usually did after breakfast. Uncle had headed to the living room and switched on the news, which began blaring through the house.

Asha stopped in the hall outside the bedroom. Ma was inside, approaching her older daughter hesitantly. "Are you married, Shona?" Ma asked.

"Yes. I am. Till death do us part. The priest made it short and quick. My husband paid the fee, and now he's home packing his suitcases for the trip."

"Well, this is not how I pictured it, but I'm so glad and proud, Shona."

Reet's face softened; Asha could see it through a gap in the curtain. "Good, Ma," Reet said. "And we can have some kind of a party when we come home for a visit. His parents want to arrange something, too, so their relatives won't feel slighted, and he agreed."

Asha went to the bathroom in a daze, her head spinning. Her sister was married to Jay. Jay was married to Reet. It was done. Irrevocable. She'd have to live with her decision for the rest of her life.

❧

Jay left for New York without a word to Asha. After his departure, Raj didn't wait for Asha to ask, he simply cut the lock on the door to the roof. Asha took her diary up there and wrote and wrote, filling the last pages of "S.K. 1974" with tiny writing, even though the year had ended months ago. Now that she couldn't talk about the constant ache of missing Baba with either Reet or Jay, she poured it out in her diary. Sometimes, though, she'd find herself sitting without writing, staring at the closed shutters across the way.

She imagined Jay arriving at the New York airport, taking a taxi to the university, meeting his professor, setting up a studio, looking for an apartment. Trying to ready a home where he would bring his bride in a few weeks' time. She wondered if he was picking out plates, sheets, towels, pillows, and what he was thinking about as he started his new life. Did the image of a girl on a roof ever come to his mind?

The days passed somehow, and still Reet wasn't speaking to Asha. Jay sent the plane ticket, and Reet and Ma began making shopping trips to prepare for Reet's journey. Uncle offered some of the money he would have spent on a wedding to buy a trousseau.

Ma and Reet accepted it and brought home new sarees, a winter coat, salwars, new underwear, a lacy nightgown, and twelve skeins of good-quality wool that Reet insisted on buying for Ma. Auntie and Grandmother fingered the nightgown and teased Reet about when she would wear it for the first time, but Asha could hardly look at it.

Only Raj guessed what Asha was feeling, and his answer was to take her outside to play catch for hours. It helped. The thwack of the ball in her palm, the perfect arc of it as she threw it into the dusk and he caught it. Again and again, to and fro they moved in a rhythm that became a silent dance. Sometimes they picked up rackets and volleyed back and forth until they'd reached a hundred and were both drenched in sweat. That helped her forget, too. For a while.

One day a letter arrived from Delhi addressed to Asha. She studied the engraved insignia in the upper left-hand corner before opening it; it was from Bishop Academy. Curious, she took it to the privacy of the bathroom to read.

My dear Asha,

We were so sorry to hear of the passing of your father. He was a dear man, and I know you must be missing him greatly. Your sister wrote to us of the news of his death, and of her upcoming marriage and move to New York. How thrilled you must be for her! A strange coincidence is that I've heard of your brother-in-law because I visit the gallery where his art is displayed quite often. A portrait that everybody was talking about was gone, but a few landscapes were there, and they were stunning. Jay Sen will be famous one day, no doubt.

Your sister thought you and your mother might be happier with a move back to Delhi. I've talked it over with our headmistress and the other faculty, and we feel it's our duty to let you finish your education here, given the circumstances. We would waive one year's tuition for you to complete your studies. Your sister also tells us that you've been tutoring in Calcutta, and that you're quite good at it. She sent along copies of your cousin's math results before and after you took him in hand. Well done, I say, Asha. Well done!

Given your talents in teaching, we want to offer you a part-time tutoring position. Many of our parents are wealthy, as you know, and eager for the academy to hire a good tutor. The parents' council decided to fund the position, and I believe the salary we can offer is decent. You would meet with students on campus every afternoon after school.

As for housing, your sister mentioned a nice

flat close to the academy, so you and your mother can start looking as soon as you get here. In the meantime, Kavita's family has offered space for you in their home. There's plenty of room for the two of you to stay as long as you desire, her mother assures me.

Last but not least, I have more good news for you. There has been discussion about expanding the psychology department here at Delhi University. They might be offering a full doctoral program soon. In a year or two, you could take the exam and apply for a scholarship in their master's program. I'll help you study, I promise.

Write soon, after you discuss these possibilities with your family, as I'll need to make the necessary arrangements. Enclosed is enough money for two one-way train tickets from Calcutta to Delhi, sent with love and affection from your teachers here at Bishop Academy.

Blessings to you and yours,
Mrs. Joshi

P.S. If you decide not to come, use the money as you wish. Knowing you, we decided you'd probably buy books.

Asha's eyes were so blurry by the end, she could barely read the postscript, which made her smile. For the first time she could look into the future and see some kind of gain.

She'd had to give up Baba, then Jay, and even her sister, but at least now she might not have to lose all of her dreams. And maybe she could even manage to keep the bossy, scolding, engaged version of their mother around, the one she loved so dearly despite all the mistakes Ma had made.

Asha took the letter and found her sister hanging laundry on the line in the garden. "Where's the washerwoman?" Asha asked. "Why are you doing that?"

"I gave her the afternoon off," Reet said coolly. "I owed her one, anyway. And I like doing laundry. What's that you've got there?"

"A letter. From Mrs. Joshi. Reet, you wrote to her even while you were furious?"

Her sister shrugged. "You're not the only one who made promises, you know. I made some, too, remember?"

Asha reached over tentatively to take her sister's hand, and this time Reet didn't pull away. "Thank you, Reet. Thank you."

"It was his idea, too. He offered to send money so that you and Ma could move out of this house before I even asked him about Delhi." Her sister still wasn't able to say Jay's name in front of Asha.

"I'm so sorry about everything, Reet," Asha said. "I've gone over it a thousand times in my mind, and I can't think of what else I could have done."

Reet handed her one of Uncle's undershirts. "Here, you may as well help. I tried to think about it from your side after I cooled down a bit, Osh, and I probably would have made the same choice. You ought to have told me first, though."

"That would have ruined everything," Asha said,

wringing the shirt as hard as she could to get the last bit of water out. "You never would have let me, Reet. Never." She pegged the vest to the line.

Reet picked up a soaking towel, and the sisters began twisting it from either end. Water splashed around their feet, and Asha was reminded of standing together in the Ganges. They had been through so much—she couldn't imagine life without her sister. But they had also known that the day of separation was inevitable as they watched their mother tuck away another bangle or their father put more rupees into their dowries. And now that day was here.

Reet was obviously thinking through her sister's decision again. "I wouldn't have told you, either," she said. "I'm still not sure it was the right choice, but there's not much we can do now."

"Thank you, Reet. Thank you for trying to understand."

They held the towel to the line, each pegging one corner. "Do you think . . . do you think he'll come around?" Reet asked.

"I don't know," Asha answered honestly. "He's furious. But not at you, Reet. And he'll treat you well, in any case."

Reet sighed. "That's what I said I wanted, didn't I? If only . . . Oh well, time will tell, I suppose. I'm actually kind of glad that I get to see New York."

Asha hesitated. Then she asked, "Will you go to *that* station?"

"Of course I will. You would, too. I want to see the place where Baba was last thinking of us, Osh."

"Oh, I'd like to see it with you."

"Maybe you can visit us. After a while." And Reet reached over to tug gently on her sister's braid.

"A long while," Asha said, smiling at the familiar gesture.

They finished wringing out and hanging the rest of the laundry in silence, but at least now the air between them wasn't fraught with hostility.

"Let's go tell Ma the news, Osh," Reet said once the bucket was empty.

"Do you think she'll want to go back to Delhi? She doesn't like Kavita's family too much."

"Are you joking? She'll do anything to get out of this house. Plus she'll have greater freedom there; Delhi's a far more modern city. We might even get her in a white saree with a colored border. Or at least visiting some of the gatherings she used to enjoy so much. Let's go ask her now."

Reet was right. Ma's face lit up when Asha read her the letter. "Delhi is the only real home I've known," she confessed. "It's where I spent my married life, where I had you girls. I've been so homesick, I can't tell you how much. And I'm dying in this house, absolutely dying."

"But what about living with Kavita's family for a while, Ma?" Reet asked. "Can you handle being there until I can send you money for rent?"

Ma smiled ruefully. "I've come down a bit since we left Delhi, girls, and it's been a good thing in some ways. Your baba used to chide me for not trusting people, and I've finally learned my lesson. You were right, Tuni, and I was wrong. That Kavita of yours *is* a good friend."

"I'll send the money as soon as I get to New York," Reet

said. "You'll be mistress of your own home again before you know it."

"What good girls your baba gave me!" Ma said, drawing both of her daughters close. "I see he's still keeping his promise to take care of me."

# THIRTY-TWO

The family's reaction to the news about Asha and Ma's move to Delhi was predictably mixed. Auntie's silence told them all that she thought it was the best idea she'd heard in a long time. Uncle, Raj, the little cousins, and Grandmother protested vehemently at first. Bit by bit, Reet, Asha, and Ma wore down their objections.

"Who is this Kavita?" Grandmother demanded.

"We've been friends for years," Asha said.

"She's the other top student at Bishop—second only to Osh," Reet added. "I mean Tuni."

"Good family. Educated. Punjabi, but so kind they almost seem Bengali." That was Ma, of course.

"And what is this teaching you'll be doing, Tuni?"

"In the school, Grandmother. Not in people's houses.

The school is paying me, so I won't have to take money from anybody's hands. I'll get a salary every month."

"The standard of living in Delhi is much better than here in Calcutta," Ma informed them, showing a flash of her old haughtiness.

"What would Bintu want?" Uncle asked.

"Baba would want Ma to make the decision," Asha answered quickly. Once her mother was no longer under her in-laws' roof, she might be able to bend the rules of widowhood enough to start enjoying life again. Tradition forbade widows to remarry, but she could still have fun, couldn't she? Ma would delight in being in charge of her own home again.

"He'd also want Asha to study," Reet added.

"My husband would say this chance was a gift from God," Ma said firmly, and Grandmother nodded her agreement, settling the matter once and for all.

Reet was scheduled to leave Calcutta a week after Ma and Asha departed, and Asha was dreading their goodbye. It was also surprisingly hard to leave behind a wailing Sita and Suma, who cried as if they'd never heard of happily-ever-after, or had stopped believing in it, at least.

And Grandmother, who kissed Asha's forehead after receiving her pronam. "You're a good girl, Tuni. You remind me so much of your baba."

Auntie embraced both Asha and Ma as though they were dearer than life itself. "Your brother-in-law will lose five kilos now that you won't be cooking for him, Sumitra."

"You'll have to learn," Ma said, smiling.

"Or maybe we'll hire another cook."

Raj rolled his eyes and bent to give his aunt pronam. He turned to Asha, and she flung open her arms. They hugged for the first time since they were little, and she couldn't keep back the tears. He had been so good to her, this cousin of hers. As good as a brother.

"Maybe *I'll* end up living under *your* roof," he said, handing her a clean handkerchief. "I'm applying to engineering programs, and they have a good one in Delhi."

She blew her nose and wiped her eyes. "Engineering? Really?"

"Now that I'm a math genius."

"But what about your other dream, Raj?"

His expression softened. "You're not the only one who can make a sacrifice, Osh," he said. "But keep that arm in shape; we have to beat our volley record the next time we see each other."

Reet and Uncle took Asha and Ma to the train station. The rest of the family stood at the gate waving, and Asha twisted her neck to keep them in sight until the taxi turned the corner.

Howrah station was even more crowded than it had been when they'd arrived, with people racing to reach their destinations before the prime minister declared a state of emergency. Nobody knew when it would happen, but it was coming soon.

The sisters walked hand in hand behind Uncle and Ma on the platform. Asha noticed their mother and uncle talking easily, both of them ignoring the curious glances from passersby who were probably wondering why a white-clad widow was chatting with a man.

"I'll miss your cooking, Sumitra," Uncle said when the time came to say goodbye. "And your stories, Tuni."

"I'll miss playing twenty-nine, Uncle."

"You'll come for a visit. I'll send the tickets as soon as things settle down a bit. Stay close to your mother, Tuni, and take care of her."

This time he did sound exactly like Baba, and after Asha gave her uncle pronam, she reached up to kiss his cheek the way she used to kiss her father's.

Uncle began directing the coolie to load the suitcases into their compartment. The conductor called out his warning of the train's departure. Asha turned to her sister, and they held each other close. "I love you, sister of mine," Reet whispered.

"Love you, too."

Ma clung to Reet as though her daughter was three years old again. "Take care, my darling girl. Be good to your husband."

"I'll try, Ma," Reet said.

Ma and Asha climbed aboard the train and stood at the open door. Reet walked beside them on the platform as the train began to move, still holding her sister's hand. Uncle followed at a distance.

"Mail a postcard as soon as you get there, Reet," Asha said. "Find something new that Baba didn't already send."

"No chance. The first one's going to have your saree-wearing twin on it. Lift that lantern high!"

They were laughing and crying as they released each other's hand. The train gathered speed and Reet tried to keep up on the platform, running as fast as she could. But she wasn't fast enough. Ma and Asha hurried to their compartment and leaned out the window: Reet and Uncle were already gone.

The other four seats in the compartment were empty. Uncle had insisted on paying for the entire compartment. "It's what my brother would do," he'd said as he bought the tickets, and Asha felt another rush of love for him as she and Ma got settled.

Ma took off her sandals and sat cross-legged, tucking her feet under her saree. She pulled out the sweater she had just started knitting for her new son-in-law. It was blue, blue like the Calcutta summer sky, like the color of the ocean that separated them now. Asha tried, and almost succeeded, not to imagine Jay wearing it.

The train slowed, and mother and daughter watched a crow rise from a banyan tree into the sky and disappear behind the clouds.

"My father was a farmer, Tuni," Ma said suddenly. "An uneducated man. We struggled to find money for food from week to week. My mother, too, was illiterate. Your baba sent them money after we got married, and we took care of them, but I was always ashamed of them. I shouldn't have been. They were wonderful people."

Asha listened quietly, feeling a pang because Reet wasn't able to hear this. Her sister deserved these revelations about the Strangers as much as she did.

"I wanted so badly to give a son to your baba, to show

him gratitude for what he had done for my parents," Ma said. "But I couldn't. And when you were born, I kept thinking what a perfect boy you would have made. You were so clever, and bright, and agile. I even had a name picked out if you had been a boy. I was going to call you Satya, which means 'truth.' "

"*If* I had been a boy," Asha repeated.

"But you weren't," Ma said simply. "You were a girl. And your baba must have known you would be, because he had a name picked out, too. A good name. A girl's name."

"Asha. Which means 'hope.' " Somewhere deep inside, Asha felt an old knot loosen, like a fist unclenching.

"And now I see that he chose perfectly. Because life without hope can be worse than death itself."

"You've got to fight hard for hope, Ma. You can't just give up."

"I'll try, Tuni. I'll do my best." And Ma started knitting again, fiercely, as if her life depended on it.

"Tell me more about our grandparents, Ma," Asha said after a while. She'd been wanting to turn the Strangers into family for so long.

Ma didn't hesitate. "Nobody could grow flowers like Baba," she said, still knitting. "His dahlias were the talk of the village. And Ma! She didn't say much, but she put her love into her cooking, even when we only had rice and dal. That's how I learned. Ma married Baba when she was only fourteen, and had me at fifteen. She was more like a sister than a mother, because I was their only child. I had a little brother, too, but he died when he was only ten months old."

*I didn't know,* Asha thought. *An uncle. I had another uncle.*

"I never found out what they named him. I wish I had. My mother didn't get out of bed for weeks. But my father knew how to comfort her. Even when I couldn't, no matter how hard I tried. Just like your father could comfort me."

Ma talked and knitted, knitted and talked, pouring untold stories into the empty compartment like a river flowing down from the Himalayas, through Calcutta, and into the sea. And Asha caught her mother's secrets, tucking them one by one into the urn of her memory.

# THIRTY-THREE

WHEN THE TAXI DROPPED THEM AT KAVITA'S HOUSE, IT WAS past midnight, but Asha's friend greeted them rapturously. "Auntie, Osh, we're so glad you're here. Is Reet really married? I can hardly believe it. I want to hear all about it."

"You must be tired, Kavi," Asha said. "It's so late. We'll talk in the morning."

Kavita's parents were waiting up also. "We're honored to have you, Sumitra. And your daughter, too. Thank you for accepting our invitation."

"Thank you so much for hosting us," Ma replied in her hesitant English.

"Oh, two packages came for you, Osh," Kavita said. "I've left them in your room. One was as heavy as a human being. I asked the servants to be extra careful with it because it was marked fragile."

After Kavita's family said good night, Ma went to take a bath and wash the traveling dust away. Asha followed a servant into the guest room, where he placed their suitcases, turned down the twin beds, and brought in a pitcher of drinking water with two glasses.

When she was finally alone, Asha took a closer look at the two packages. The smaller one was from Calcutta, and Reet's handwriting was all over it. Her sister must have sent it a week or so ago for it to arrive before they did.

The other, much larger package had been sent by courier from a gallery in Delhi. Asha could guess what was inside, but she opened her sister's gift first. It was a diary, with a key, just like the ones Baba had always found. Asha hugged and kissed it as though it were alive.

"Nineteen seventy-five, at last," she whispered.

She turned to the heavy, flat package that was leaning against a wall. Carefully removing the brown paper and twine, she set it all aside neatly and didn't peek until it was fully uncovered.

Then, and only then, she allowed herself to see it.

And lost her breath.

It was Asha Gupta.

But not really.

Or maybe it was.

Jay had sent a portrait of a young woman on a Calcutta roof, dressed in a moss-green salwar kameez embroidered with tiny white flowers, her silky, sunlit hair tousled by the wind. She was graceful, lovely, her expression so sweet it hurt Asha to look at it. But the girl had power, too, a strength that was obvious in the line of her jaw, the bend of her elbow, the fingers that clutched the pen tightly.

The entire canvas was painted with such care and detail that Asha felt as if she, too, were forced to gaze with love and desire at this unknown young woman. Just as the painter must have.

The name of the portrait was engraved across the bottom of the frame. *The Secret,* Jay had titled it, and Asha knew she would keep it forever.

# AUTHOR'S NOTE

I WAS BORN IN KOLKATA, INDIA, THE CITY WHERE MOST OF Asha's story takes place, to parents who migrated there from East Bengal (now Bangladesh) during the 1947 partition of India and Pakistan. The U.S. National Origins Act of 1965 raised the quota of Asian immigrants to twenty thousand people a year, matching the number admitted from European countries. However, most Indian professionals only started coming in the 1970s—as did my father, who headed to New York to seek an engineering job. Unlike Asha, I joined him, along with my mother and two older sisters, when I was seven years old. I became an American citizen when I was seventeen.

The country of my birth was ruled by the British for two centuries before winning independence in 1947 (immediately followed by the above-mentioned partition), so India's schools, government, hospitals, roads, and railroads are modeled after the United Kingdom's. Even today, Indians use English as an informal lingua franca and learn it in school along with Hindi, the official national language. Most also speak yet another language as their mother tongue, one of the twenty-one major languages or dozens of regional dialects.

The 1970s were a difficult time for India's young democracy. The country's army fought and defeated Pakistan's army in 1971 at great cost, crops failed in 1972 and 1973, and industries followed suit thanks to skyrocketing world oil prices during 1973 and 1974. Prime Minister Indira Gandhi's government, struggling to stay in power and keep the country from disintegrating into conflict, took over the banks, passed strict land reform laws, and moved the country toward socialism. India drew closer to Russia and moved away from America. With strikes and civil disobedience on the rise, Gandhi declared a state of national emergency in June 1977, and suspended civil rights for almost two years. The government threw thousands of people into prison, forced many to be sterilized against their will, froze wages, and evicted urban squatters and slum dwellers. *Secret Keeper* is set in that time of uncertainty and chaos.

Indian cities today are completely different places, thanks to new technologies, an educated workforce, and an increasingly open economic climate. Women are entering the job market in droves, and urban young people creatively fuse imported cultural practices with age-old Indian customs.

Rural areas, however, are slow to change. Some of the traditions described in this novel still regulate life in Hindu villages of Bengal. Elders are honored and cared for at home by sons, daughters-in-law, and grandchildren. The closeness of joint families provides community and prevents loneliness.

But some age-old customs make life difficult for village girls and women. Some widows, no matter their age, are expected to dress in white, give up meat, eggs, and fish, and never remarry. When a girl has her first period, she loses the freedom to roam and play and must meet rigid new expectations for her behavior and appearance. Teenagers marry men who are usually five or more years older, and some village girls bring dowries when they move to their inlaws' homes. The marriage of an older sister is still arranged first, with exceptions proving the rule, and families pick husbands and set wedding dates after consulting astrologers. In some places, lighter skin tones continue to be overvalued, and when a third daughter like me is born to a sonless family, families still grieve.

This story was written after many teatime conversations with my parents, who freely reminisced with humor and tears as I gained insight into my heritage. Their stories enriched my imagination, and I am deeply indebted. My mother, for example, mentioned a rooftop conversation she had once with a handsome next-door neighbor. When the servants tattled to my grandmother, the door to the roof was locked and Ma's window boarded up. As I listened, the character of Jay came leaping into my mind. I also give thanks for my two older sisters, as precious to me as Reet is to Asha, and for my husband and sons, who give me the space and grace to write.

# TUNTUNI AND THE WICKED CAT
## A BENGALI FOLKTALE

*In* Secret Keeper, *Asha Gupta recounts several Tuntuni stories to her extended family. This one is retold and elaborated by Mitali Perkins, but was originally written by Upendra Kishore Roy in* Tuntunir Bai, *1910.*

Once upon a time Tuntuni bird wanted to lay her eggs. She found an eggplant tree in the back garden and built a cozy nest by stitching the plant's leaves together. Soon two small baby birds were asleep in the nest. They were so small they couldn't fly or even open their eyes. They would just open their mouths and call out "cheen-cheen, cheen-cheen" when they were hungry.

Those baby birds were safe, thanks to the thorns on the stems of the eggplant. But there were plenty of hungry animals around, so Tuntuni watched over them carefully.

Of all the animals, the cat was the most wicked, the most prideful, and the most greedy. Every day he ignored the delicious sweet milk he was given and prowled the garden instead, gazing up at the eggplant tree, thinking, *If only I could eat Tuntuni's babies.* All he wanted was one juicy bite of those two small birds, and the feel of them gulping, gulping, gulping down his throat.

One day he came close, very, very close indeed, and asked in a careful meow, "What are you doing, dear Tuntuni?"

Tuntuni thought quickly. She knew that the cat was hungry for attention—almost more than he wanted food. She stayed on the branch close to her babies and bowed her head, saying, "What an honor to have you visit, Your Highness. I feel as though the king himself has come to see us. And what beautiful thick golden fur you have. Oh, and those whiskers! Magnificent!"

The cat went away happy—for a time, until the thought of those two juicy babies pushed away the good feeling of Tuntuni's praises. The next day, he came again, very, very close indeed, and eyed the sleeping fledglings. Staying close to the nest, Tuntuni bowed low, addressed the cat as "King," and showered him with more praise and admiration. Again and again the cat went away feeling happy, even though his tummy still growled.

Bit by bit, Tuntuni's fledglings grew up, until they no longer kept their eyes shut. Soon their mother asked them, "My dear ones, can you fly now?"

The little ones answered, "Yes, Ma, we can."

Tuntuni said, "Let's see if you can hop over to the top branch of that tall coconut tree."

The fledglings immediately flew over to the top branch.

Tuntuni flapped her wings in delight, smiled, and said, "Let the evil cat come now!"

After a while, the cat strolled over and said, "So, what are you up to, Tuntuni?"

He was expecting her usual royal treatment, but Tuntuni was done with that game. The bird flew low, threw a kick at the cat's head, and said, "Get lost, you wretched creature!" Then she quickly darted away.

Snarling in rage, the cat jumped on the eggplant tree, but the nest was gone, and the thorns scratched him. He tried to climb the coconut tree, but it was so tall, he couldn't reach either Tuntuni or the babies.

With his tail between his legs, the cat returned to his bowl of now sour milk.

# GLOSSARY

*Here are some Bangla words that you may already understand after reading* Secret Keeper.

**BANGLA**: The national language of Bangladesh, also spoken in West Bengal, a state in India, and the fourth most widely spoken language in the world. It's sometimes called Bengali, but the official name is Bangla. Literature and poetry are written in high Bangla, while villagers in different corners of Bengal speak dialects that differ in tone and grammar.

**BENGALI**: An ethnic term used to identify Indians who originated in Bengal and speak Bangla.

**BETA**: A term of affection for a son.

**BHAGAVAN**: A name for the personal God.

**CHANACHOOR**: A spicy, crunchy mix of fried lentils, nuts, and other goodies.

**CRICKET**: Considered the second most popular sport on the planet, this game is played by two teams of eleven players on an oval grass field. In the center of the field is a flat strip of ground 22 yards (20.12 meters) long called a cricket pitch.

A wicket, usually made of wood, is placed at each end of the pitch. A bowler from the fielding team, standing by one wicket, throws a hard, fist-sized ball toward the other wicket. The ball usually bounces once before reaching the batsman, a player from the opposing team, who defends the wicket with his wooden bat. Meanwhile, the other members of the bowler's team stand around the field to retrieve the ball in an effort to stop the batsman from scoring runs and to get him out.

**DAK NAM**: A nickname given to every Bengali child used at home by the extended family. Asha's dak nam is Tuni, Reet's is Shona, and Raj is called Beta by his parents.

**DAL**: Slow-cooked lentils with spices.

**DOWRY**: The gift of money, jewelry, clothing, and sometimes furniture given by a bride's family to the groom's family at the time of their marriage.

**EESH!**: Depending on the speaker's tone of voice, this Bangla exclamation means that something either shameful, disappointing, or disastrous has happened.

**HARMONIUM**: A hand-pumped reed organ played by the musician sitting cross-legged on the floor behind the instrument. This was introduced by British missionaries to India in the mid-nineteenth century and became popular in Bengal.

**KOLKATA**: A large city on the east coast of India in the state of West Bengal. The British used to call it Calcutta, but India changed the official spelling in 2001.

**KURTA**: Boys and men wear this knee-length shirt over loose drawstring trousers called pajama.

**LUCHI**: Round, soft, puffy bread made of fine flour, water, and salt and fried in hot oil.

**PANTHUA**: Spongy brown balls of sweetened cottage cheese drenched in syrup. A traditional Bengali sweet.

**POISHA** or **PAISE**: An Indian coin worth a hundredth of a rupee.

**PRONAM**: A greeting given to elders and important people, by bending to touch their feet with the hand and then one's own forehead.

**RICKSHAW**: A small two-wheeled vehicle used as a taxi. Sometimes it's pulled by a human being who pedals a cycle attached to the seat carrying passengers, but if an engine is used to power it, the vehicle is called an auto-rickshaw or baby taxi.

**RUPEE**: The official currency of India. One dollar was equal to forty-one rupees at the time of this writing.

**SALWAR KAMEEZ**: Girls wear this three-piece outfit, which consists of a kameez, a long shirt or tunic; a salwar, or loose pajamalike trousers; and a dupatta, a long scarf or shawl.

**SAMOSA**: Fried triangular pastry shells stuffed with a savory filling of spiced potatoes, onion, peas, coriander, and sometimes meat or lentils.

**SAREE**: A long garment made of five to six yards of cloth that a woman wraps, pleats, and tucks around her waist and then drapes over her shoulder. It's usually worn over a tight-fitting blouse and a petticoat.

**TIK-TIKI**: A small, harmless house lizard.

**TWENTY-NINE**: A popular card game involving bids and trumps played in parts of India by two teams of two people each.

# ACKNOWLEDGMENTS

Many thanks to editor Françoise Bui for understanding my life between cultures, agent Laura Rennert for stewarding my writing dreams, the members of my writers' group for eagle-eyed critiques, my loving family (including the dear ones in Kolkata), and, last but never least, the Keeper of my secrets, who is taking me from start to finish.

# ABOUT THE AUTHOR

MITALI PERKINS (whose first name means "friendly" in Bangla) was born in Kolkata. The Bose family was always on the move, leaving India for Ghana, Cameroon, England, New York, and Mexico. They finally settled in California, where Mitali grew up.

After her marriage, Mitali's travels continued, and the Perkins family lived in India, Bangladesh, and Thailand before putting down roots in Massachusetts. The third daughter in her family of origin, Mitali now thrives in an otherwise all-male household (husband, two sons, two Labs, and one ferret).

Mitali's previous young adult novels include *Monsoon Summer, The Not-So-Star-Spangled Life of Sunita Sen*, and the companion First Daughter books, as well as *Rickshaw Girl,* a story for younger readers. She maintains a Web site (www.mitaliperkins.com) and a blog (mitaliblog.com), where she chats about books, movies, music, television, and life between cultures.